Praise for

Risk Factor
The Fourth Buddy Steel Thriller

"The perfect substitute for that good-time trip to California you've decided not to take after all."

—*Kirkus Reviews*

"Screenwriter Brandman uses snappy dialogue to keep the pace quick and the action kinetic. This series is a natural for TV adaptation."

—*Publishers Weekly*

"Vivid characters, a flawed but very likable hero who exudes grit, a meaty plot with plenty of twists, and a satisfying ending make this a thoroughly enjoyable read."

—*Booklist*

Wild Card
The Third Buddy Steel Thriller

"Brandman's fast and fun third Buddy Steel mystery... Buddy shines as an investigator, tough guy, and observer of the human condition."

—*Publishers Weekly*

"Another irreverent, complex lawman."

—*Library Journal*

"Readers who enjoy action and attitude will find much to enjoy in Buddy's third adventure."

—*Booklist*

One on One
The Second Buddy Steel Thriller

"Another great read. Buddy Steel is my kind of sheriff."

—Tom Selleck

"Buddy is a likable character who uses self-deprecating humor, sometimes acting like an overgrown schoolboy. He is easygoing and can handle people poking fun at him. Being smart, caring, and understanding of people's emotional pain, Buddy has a moral sense of right versus wrong. Readers will enjoy this fast-paced mystery. With well-developed characters and a plot that takes issues straight from the headlines, this is a good read."

—*Crimespree Magazine*

Missing Persons
The First Buddy Steel Thriller

"*Missing Persons* is a cracking series debut and Buddy Steel is a protagonist bound to have a long shelf life."

—Reed Farrel Coleman, *New York Times* bestselling author of *What You Break*

"Fans of Parker's work will appreciate Buddy, another irreverent, complex lawman."

—*Library Journal*

"Michael Brandman's follow-up to the three Jesse Stone novels he adeptly penned for the late Robert B. Parker gives us the cool and iconic Buddy Steel. A former point guard turned cop, Steel damn sure owns the ground he walks on. All capable 6'3" and 170 pounds of him, Buddy's that guy that you want to ride with when s..t hits the fan. With plenty of thrilling moments and turns you don't see coming, what a great ride Brandman takes us on in *Missing Persons*. Trust me, you won't be disappointed. Buckle up."

—Robert Knott, *New York Times* bestselling
author of the Hitch and Cole Series

Also by Michael Brandman

The Buddy Steel Thrillers
Missing Persons
One on One
Wild Card
Risk Factor

The Jesse Stone Novels
Robert B. Parker's Fool Me Twice
Robert B. Parker's Killing the Blues
Robert B. Parker's Damned If You Do

DEATH THREAT

DEATH THREAT

A BUDDY STEEL THRILLER

MICHAEL BRANDMAN

Poisoned Pen
PRESS

Published by Poisoned Pen Press, an imprint of Sourcebooks
P.O. Box 4410, Naperville, Illinois 60567-4410
(630) 961-3900
sourcebooks.com

Cataloging-in-Publication data is on file with the Library of Congress.

Printed and bound in the United States of America.
SB 10 9 8 7 6 5 4 3 2 1

For Joanna...

... Night and Day
You are the one ...

PROLOGUE

The obituary appeared in Sunday's edition of the *Los Angeles Times.*

LAPD DEPUTY COMMANDER JEREMY LOGAN DIES AT 77

It caught me by surprise and brought unexpected tears to my eyes.

Jeremy Logan.

My mentor and champion.

Gone.

My first instinct was to pick up the phone and call Kara Machado, but I realized I had no idea where she might be. Nor what I might say, should I even find her.

By way of introduction, I'm Buddy Steel.

Actually Burton Steel Jr., but I don't especially cotton to the name Burton. Or Burt. Or Junior.

Back in my high school days, a couple of pals called me Buddy. And it stuck.

My thoughts turned to Commander Jeremy Logan.

He was the first senior officer to take notice of me, a crusty veteran who saw something in a twenty-five-year-old rookie cop and took the time to nurture and commend him.

There are so many Logan stories. He was such a great character.

But there's one linchpin story that changed my life. And it's never far from my thoughts. I remember it as if it took place yesterday.

And I can't resist telling it.

So bear with me.

I had been with the LAPD for just over a year when I applied for detective status.

I had just finished my shift when I spotted the commander, who was making a rare appearance at the Hollywood station.

When he caught my eye, Jeremy Logan motioned for me to join him in the conference room.

Never one for hyperbole, Logan threw his heavy arm around my shoulder and growled, "I signed off on your appointment."

"Excuse me?"

"It was you applied for detective status, wasn't it? There's not another Buddy Steel on the force, is there?"

I smiled at his joke.

"You won't hear officially for a couple more days, so try to act surprised when they tell you."

This was a dream come true for me. I was tongue-tied. "I don't know what to say."

"You could try, 'Thanks,' for openers."

"Thanks for openers."

"Funny. Do your best not to make me look like a schmuck, okay, Buddy?"

He winked and flashed me his toothy grin. He was a tall man, six feet plus, marginally overweight, and more than slightly out of shape, a victim of the stress level that accompanied the job.

"I'm very proud of you," he said. "You've got a great future in front of you."

I could feel my face reddening.

"You want anything, you let me know," Logan said, punching me playfully in the shoulder. "And don't be surprised if I cook up some special assignments for you."

Little did I know he had already cooked up something that tested me in ways that informed my entire career.

ONE

I awakened in a cold sweat, one tinged with apprehension and fear. The dream had returned. Nearly two years later and it haunted me still.

In the dream, I find myself standing barefoot and stock-still on a street corner in downtown Los Angeles. It's brutally hot. I'm surrounded by hordes of people, all of them rushing every which way.

I spot my mother in the crowd. She's wearing only a nightgown and appears confused. Lost. Ill. I call out to her, but no sound crosses my lips.

I chase after her, my shoeless feet burning on the scorching pavement. But no matter how fast I run, she remains beyond my grasp. I see her turn a corner, but when I arrive there, she's vanished.

I sat up in bed, breathing heavily, staring blankly into space.

I remembered the first time I awakened from the same dream. I was fifteen, and my mother heard me gasping for breath and had rushed to my side.

She was already showing the early signs of her dementia, but she understood the psychological nature of the dream.

I was not yet a man, but was no longer a boy. We were close, mother and son. More so because my father was immersed in his work and frequently not at home.

I stood at the bathroom sink gulping handfuls of water. I splashed my face.

It was three fifteen. I'd slept for four hours. I would sleep no more.

I gazed at Cooper, who sat staring at me. "What are you looking at?"

Cooper didn't say anything.

I had inherited the black-and-tan bloodhound when my mother entered the home.

She and the dog had been inseparable, but she was forced to give him up according to the rules of the facility.

Now he was mine. A constant reminder of her. I pulled on my sweats and laced up my Nikes.

With Cooper leashed to my side, I stepped into the chill of the Hollywood night.

I did some stretches. I took several deep breaths.

Together with the feisty bloodhound, I ran.

The streets were deserted. We headed south toward Sunset, and when we reached the boulevard, we went west.

My tensions eased as I hit stride.

The rush of fresh air swept the lingering dream from my mind.

———

By seven, I was sitting in the Denny's at Gower Gulch, having breakfast with my partner, Philip Dinn.

We had teamed up a year ago, when I reached Officer Second

Grade status. At forty-five, twenty years my senior, Phil took me under his wing and counseled me, helping me find a measure of stability and maturity.

We were already on our second cups of coffee. "By the way," Phil said, "you look like shit."

"That's an attractive image."

The waitress brought our food. Pancakes, sausages, and three eggs for Phil. An egg white omelet for me. No toast. Also a takeout package of sausage and eggs for Cooper, who was asleep at my feet.

Phil proceeded to smear several gobs of butter on his pancakes. Then he poured a prodigious amount of maple syrup over them. He looked up at me and grinned.

"That should give the old ticker a jolt," I needled.

"Hey, I'm still a growing boy."

"Yeah, but in which direction?"

Phil had softened in recent years. He didn't exercise as much as he used to, and his physique bore the added weight of a mostly sedentary lifestyle. He showed his age, and his diminished agility had begun to worry me. "You should eat more healthfully," I said.

"I'm not so overweight."

"Oh, yeah? Then why is the top button on your pants always undone?"

"Fashion statement."

"Keep telling yourself that, blimp boy."

"I resemble that remark," Phil said, shoveling a heaping forkful of pancakes into his mouth.

We ate in silence for a while. Then I asked, "You hear anything yet?"

Phil shook his head.

He signaled to the waitress for more coffee. She refilled both of our cups and dropped two checks on the table.

"Just that things are seriously tense," he said.

"Do you really believe they're gonna riot?"

"Jeez, I sure hope not," Phil said.

We paid our respective tabs and left the restaurant. Once outside, I opened the takeout package and set it down in front of Cooper, who gobbled it within seconds.

"Lucky you got your hand out of the way," Phil said. "Never trust a bloodhound around food."

I knelt down and scratched the big dog's ears, which Cooper loved. "Pay no attention to the nasty fat man."

We dropped Cooper off at my apartment, then went to work.

———

There was an extra edge of anxiety in the air as the Hollywood Division patrol officers gathered in the squad room for roll call.

The brutal killing of three black men by four LAPD officers had been at the top of the news for days.

At first the officers denied the charge, but a witness with an iPhone produced a video of the slayings, revealing a ruthless, senseless act that amounted to the equivalent of cold-blooded murders.

In South Central there were already signs of civil unrest. Tensions were high. Extra police personnel had been deployed, which had further inflamed the locals.

As it was with all of us, I feared the havoc an incident of civil disobedience could wreak. The toll it would take, not only on the force, but on the populace as well.

When Sergeant Kenny Murphy finished calling the roll and reading the morning announcements, the Hollywood Division officers filed out, each cognizant of the fact that by shift's end, conditions might have changed drastically.

TWO

Phil and I pulled into Wilcox Avenue, heading for Hollywood Boulevard.

Phil was driving, but not nearly fast enough to satisfy me. "Think you could kick it up a notch, Grandpa?"

"Hey, if you think you can do better, you're welcome to take the wheel."

"And if I said yes?"

"Yes, what?"

"Yes, I'll take the wheel."

"Let me tell you something, boyo. On your finest day, you still couldn't hold a candle to my driving."

Before I could respond, the cruiser's radio phone announced an armed robbery taking place at a convenience store on the corner of Franklin and Cahuenga.

I looked at Phil, who activated the response button on the radio. "Car 23 en route."

"Roger, 23," the dispatcher said.

"ETA less than five."

"Copy that."

Phil switched on the siren and light bar. We raced to the site.

———

The pistol shots sent us diving for cover.

We were in hot pursuit of the gunman suspected of having robbed the convenience store.

He had led us into the alley behind the store, where he unfortunately found himself confronted by a dead end.

The alley abutted a concrete wall that offered no escape for the hapless criminal, who had secreted himself behind an overflowing dumpster and was firing his pistol at us.

I had already backed myself against the wall adjacent to the dumpster.

Phil was running toward me when one of the gunman's shots caught him in the thigh.

He stumbled, but his momentum propelled him to safety.

I hurriedly knelt beside him and examined the wound, which had started to bleed.

"Motherfucker," Phil said, grimacing in pain. "Hurts like a son of a bitch."

I removed my uniform shirt and, in an effort to stanch the bleeding, tied it as tightly as I could around Phil's thigh. He grunted.

"You okay?" I asked.

"Don't worry about me."

"It's actually my shirt I'm worried about."

Phil smiled weakly.

I handed him my cell phone. "Call it in. I'm going to take this asshole down."

I inched my way around the dumpster.

Sensing movement, the shooter cried out. "I surrender."

When I didn't respond, the gunman hollered, "I'm going to throw down my gun."

A small-caliber pistol skittered along the ground and came to a stop in front of the dumpster.

"Now I'm unarmed."

"Step out with your hands in the air," I instructed.

The gunman stepped tentatively from behind the dumpster, his hands above his head. He appeared to be in his early twenties, dressed in unwashed jeans and a hooded sweatshirt. The smirk on his face was far too smug for my taste. I moved toward him, my service weapon, a Colt Commander .45 semiautomatic pistol, pointed at his head.

"I'm not armed," the gunman bellowed.

"You shot a police officer. You do realize that no one would blame me if I killed you on the spot."

"I said I surrender."

"Unaccepted."

"What do you mean, unaccepted?"

"You have to answer for shooting my partner."

"Fuck you, asswipe. I already threw down my gun."

"No respect," I said, slowly shaking my head.

I holstered my weapon, grabbed the gunman by his shirt collar, and put everything I had into a punch to his jaw that sent him reeling.

The gunman screamed. He grabbed his face. Blood leaked onto his hands. "You broke my jaw," he whined.

"You think?" I said as I grabbed the man's left wrist and cuffed it.

"I wasn't even armed."

"You made a move toward me," I said, as I cuffed his other wrist.

"I didn't make no move toward you."

"Who do you think is gonna believe that?"

"You're a fucking liar."

"Tell it to the judge."

THREE

The ambulance carrying Phil Dinn sped away first.

The second, carrying the gunman, left shortly thereafter.

I stood in the alley, talking with Lieutenant Abel Persky, my superior officer.

"Fractured jaw," Persky said. "He'll be spitting out remnants of teeth for days."

I enjoyed that image. "What did the medics say?"

"About Phil?"

"Yeah."

"He should be okay. He'll be out for a while, though."

"What's a while?"

"Bullet ripped up his thigh pretty good. He's likely looking at a fair measure of physiotherapy."

We walked toward my cruiser.

"You gonna want to work alone while he's out?" Persky asked.

"Jesus, Abe, he just got shot. I haven't even absorbed that yet. Besides, I believe it's your call anyway."

"When do you learn the results of the test?"

"The detective test?"

"Yeah."

"They're saying this week."

"Homicide?"

"It's what I applied for. I hate it that Phil got shot like that."

"At least he's gonna recover."

"I hope so. He's not exactly a spring chicken, you know."

"Shelley Hartman is looking for a partner," Persky said.

"Hartman the Heartless?"

"You know her?"

"Know of."

"I'll ask her to look you up at call."

"Okay."

"You're gonna have to deal with Internal Affairs."

"Because?"

"You'll have to explain how it came about you shattered the perp's jaw."

"I hit him, that's how."

"I know you hit him. The question is why."

"Self-defense. Guy threatened me."

"Threatened you how?"

"He looked like he was about to rush me."

"Rush you?"

"That's what it looked like."

"Like he was going to assault you?"

"Yes."

"With his fists?"

"Yes."

"Why didn't you just shoot him?"

"He was unarmed."

"So you slugged him instead?"

"I did."

"Because you thought he was going to attack you with his fists?"

"Correct."

"Why would he do a thing like that?" Persky asked.

"Beats me," I replied.

FOUR

I pulled the cruiser into the parking lot behind Hollywood Division headquarters, and flipped the keys to the attendant who would refuel and inspect the vehicle before turning it over to the next shift.

I headed to the squad room for roll call. The new shift officers were about to take over. Nothing had been reported regarding the possibility of a full-blown riot.

The names were just being called when I entered and took a seat in the back. Having heard of my takedown of the alleged assailant, several officers greeted me with inquiring eyes.

Before the shift was dismissed, Sergeant Kenny Murphy's gaze settled on me. "See me after, will you, Buddy?" he said.

I nodded.

The meeting broke up, and the new shift officers hurriedly departed for duty. I was heading in Sergeant Murphy's direction when I spotted a spirited female officer approaching me.

"Shelley Hartman," she said, extending her hand. "Pleased to meet you," I said, grasping it.

"Likewise. Abe mentioned you might need to partner up for a spell."

I shrugged.

"Is that a yes shrug or a no shrug?"

"A little of both."

"Meaning?"

"Yes and no."

"I think I'm developing a headache," Hartman said. In her mid to late twenties, Shelley Hartman was a force of nature. Tall, toned, and stunning, she exuded self-confidence.

"I've never worked with a woman before."

"And you're horrified at the prospect, right?"

"Horrified?"

"I knew it," she said.

"You're some kind of wiseass, aren't you?"

"Why, whatever do you mean?"

"Are you any good?"

"Would you like a copy of my résumé?"

"Okay."

"Okay, what?"

"Let's try it."

"Let's try it?"

"Yes."

"Am I supposed to be flattered or something? You know, you don't exactly possess the most stellar reputation."

"I never said I did."

"Okay," she said.

"Okay, what?"

"I'll see you tomorrow morning at eight."

"You drive," I said.

"You'd let a woman drive?"

"I'm sure I'll live to regret it."

We were interrupted by Sergeant Murphy, who called out, "Steel."

"Tomorrow," Hartman said.

She stared at me for a moment, then left the squad room.

I walked over to Kenny Murphy. "Murph," I said.

"Phil okay?"

"Nothing the loss of fifteen pounds wouldn't cure."

"I mean his leg."

"He's got some serious rehabbing in front of him."

"I hear you fractured the guy's jaw."

"He needed subduing."

"Subduing?"

"He looked like he was about to attack me."

Murphy looked at me. "If you say so. You have an appointment with Eleanor Berezin."

"IA?"

"Yes."

"When?"

"Now."

"Now?"

"Fast, huh?"

"I'll say."

"Somebody upstairs must want this thing expedited," Murphy said.

I, too, wondered how and why Internal Affairs got hold of this matter so quickly.

"You're gonna want to watch your mouth with her."

"I always watch my mouth."

"Except when you're running it," Murphy said.

FIVE

I wandered the halls of Parker Center in search of Eleanor Berezin's suite. Once I found it, I opened the door, which led me into an outer office that was unoccupied. I stepped inside and closed the door behind me.

From inside her office, Eleanor Berezin called out. "Officer Steel?"

I stuck my head in her door. "Ma'am."

Berezin looked up from the chaotic stack of paperwork piled high on her desk. She half stood to greet me. "Please come in. Have a seat."

I took the chair opposite her.

She was a handsome woman, in a charcoal-gray business suit worn over an open-necked white blouse. Pants, no skirt. No makeup. Short salt-and-pepper hair framed her narrow face.

She reached for one of the files and placed it in front of her. She opened it and read the top sheet. Then she looked up at me. "Just for your information, we're examining an excessive use of force issue."

I gazed at her warily. "Are you suggesting what happened today was an instance of excessive use of force?"

"You fractured a man's jaw."

"He fired his weapon at me. He shot my partner."

"Be that as it may, you violently attacked him." Her attitude and her tone caught my attention. "The victim claims he was unarmed when you struck him," she said.

I stared at her, blank-eyed.

"Do you disagree?" she asked.

I had learned early in life that in times of strife, it's often better to remain silent.

When I didn't respond, she looked away and read again from the file. "Will you describe for me what happened today?"

"The suspect opened fire on me and my partner, Philip Dinn."

"Was he provoked into firing at you?"

"Provoked?"

"Yes."

"What kind of question is that?"

"Please answer it."

"Was he provoked into firing at two police officers who were chasing him because he had just committed a robbery and was running from the scene of the crime?"

"It hasn't been proven that he robbed the convenience store."

"It hasn't been proven the tooth fairy doesn't exist either."

"Don't be flippant with me, sir."

"I don't mean to be flippant, ma'am. But you do realize this situation, as it was developing, was seriously dangerous."

Eleanor Berezin glared at me.

"The perp led us into an alley that dead-ended, firing at us as he did so. One of his shots struck Officer Dinn in the thigh."

"This so-called perp claims he threw down his weapon and surrendered."

"That's what he claims?"

"He says that regardless of his surrender, you brutally attacked him with your fists. And as a result, his lawyers are threatening suit."

"His lawyers?"

"He was provided with defense counsel who claims his client was unnecessarily brutalized by you."

"That's a load of crap."

"Language, please, Officer Steel."

"This moron did indeed throw down a weapon. And when he stepped out from behind the dumpster, his hands were in the air. But he was moving in my direction...menacingly, I might add. So rather than shoot him, I chose to disable him."

"By fracturing his jaw with your fists."

"That's right. Yes."

The door to Berezin's outer office opened. I spotted Police Commander Jeremy Logan standing in the doorway. "May I come in?" he asked.

For a moment, Berezin looked stricken. Then she nodded for him to enter.

I stood to greet him.

"Officer Steel," Logan said in his familiar growl. We shook hands.

Logan was a presence, a thirty-plus-year veteran of the department, who started as a street cop and worked his way up to deputy commander.

He was jacketless, in a white dress shirt with the medals of his rank pinned to the chest pocket.

Age and stress had etched deep grooves into his forehead, but he was still handsome, and his striking green eyes radiated intelligence and warmth.

Logan reached across the desk and shook hands with Eleanor Berezin.

"I trust you're being kind to Officer Steel," Logan said. "He appears to have gone through some kind of hell, but despite his partner having been seriously wounded, he managed to bring down the perp with a minimum of damage."

"The perp doesn't quite see it that way," Berezin replied.

"Really?" Logan said.

"He's suing."

"Yeah, well, good luck with that."

He turned to me and said, "I heard you were in the building. I wanted to stop by to say thank you."

I smiled at him.

"It's always good to remind the shitheels there are consequences for their behavior."

Then to Eleanor Berezin he said, "You understand, don't you? Thanks to Officer Steel, this particular piece of detritus will be drinking his dinner through a straw for a while. A message that also won't be lost on his associates."

I glanced briefly at Eleanor Berezin to gauge how she was reacting to Commander Logan.

"You think Officer Steel acted appropriately?" she asked.

Logan looked at her. "There's not a court in the land that would find him guilty. The perp was lucky he wasn't killed."

Berezin stared at him, shaking her head.

"You wait, Eleanor," Logan said. "Five bucks'll get you ten it never goes to trial."

"You're on," she said.

Logan winked at her.

Then he turned his attention back to me.

"You did exceptionally well on your test," Logan said. "I'm looking forward to welcoming you into my division come June first."

Logan smiled and then stood.

I stood also. "Thank you, sir."

Logan wrapped me in a bear hug.

"We're expecting big things from you, Steel."

"I'll do my best, sir."

"I know you will."

Logan smiled, then glanced at his watch. "Sorry for the intrusion," he said to Eleanor Berezin. "Look out for our young man, here. He's one of the bright lights on the commissioner's radar screen."

Logan flashed his toothy grin. Then he left.

Eleanor Berezin sat staring at me.

"That was nice of him," I said.

"I wonder how he knew this inquiry was taking place," she said.

"I wouldn't know."

"I'm sure you wouldn't know," she said.

After several moments, I said, "I guess it's good to have friends in high places."

"Excuse me?"

"You know. The song."

"What song?"

"The Garth Brooks song, 'I've Got Friends in High Places,'" I said.

"The Garth Brooks song is called, 'I've Got Friends in *LOW* Places.'"

"Really?" I exclaimed with a smile.

Finally, she smiled back and said, "Really."

"Low places. Yikes."

"Exactly," she said. "Thank you for your cooperation."

She closed my folder and placed it back on the pile. "I'll phone you if I have any further questions."

"Thank you, Ms. Berezin. I'm happy to help."

"I'm sure you are."

I reached over and shook her hand. Then I hightailed it out of there as fast as I could.

SIX

I was living in what at one time had been an upscale Hollywood residential dwelling, on the corner of Wilcox and Selma Avenues, two blocks from the Hollywood police station.

The neighborhood, once a favorite of film industry luminaries, had fallen on hard times, but the building was still reasonably well maintained.

I had found an affordable two-bedroom apartment on the top floor, one that offered a fair amount of sunlight and a modicum of quiet.

I did most of the restoration work myself and outfitted it sparingly with rustic, Mission-style furniture and accessories. It was my sanctuary, and I cherished it.

When I got home, I found Jimmy Granger, my thirteen-year-old downstairs neighbor, sprawled on the daybed in the guest room, reading my worn copy of John Steinbeck's *East of Eden*.

Cooper was lying beside him.

Jimmy was a middle school student who lived in the building with his older sister and his single mother.

He and I had bonded, and in the absence of his father, the role of surrogate father befell me. I mentored the boy, counseling and encouraging him as best I could, and guiding him when necessary.

Jimmy found solace in my apartment, where he frequently sought solitude and quiet. He looked after Cooper in the afternoons when he got home from school. "I already walked him," he said.

"Thanks."

I removed my service belt and weapon and put them away in my room. Then I returned and sat opposite him.

"Looks like you've made a big dent," I said.

"I have. I'm on page four hundred and seventy."

"Wow."

Jimmy was a good-looking kid, smart and motivated.

As was his custom, he was wearing jeans and a blue Dodgers hoodie. His unlaced high-tops were lying on the floor. "Despite the fact it takes place in the middle ages, I'm really liking it."

"The middle ages?"

"Yeah. Your era. The geezer decades."

"The geezer decades? It came out in the 1950s."

"I rest my case."

"But you like it?"

"I do."

"More so than *Gatsby*?"

"Different."

"It's my favorite."

"I know."

"Have you started the report?"

"I've been keeping notes. Like you suggested. I'm hoping to finish it by the weekend and then start writing the paper."

The apartment door opened, and Betty Jean Granger stepped in.

"Oh, Buddy," she said when she spotted me, "I'm sorry to just barge in like this. I didn't realize you were here."

"It's okay, Betty Jean."

"I came to fetch Jimmy."

"It's okay."

Betty Jean was the type of woman I had always found attractive. Her thick hair was cut short and framed her slender face with an unruly riot of auburn. Her arresting brown eyes reflected smarts and humor. She was full-breasted and zaftig.

At thirty-six, eleven years my senior, she was assertive and self-assured, vivacious and energetic, although lately she had begun to show signs of the freight she bore as the sole parent to a pair of adolescents.

She worked as a legal secretary at a nearby entertainment law firm. She earned extra money by having secured a notary public license. Her ex was a CPA who had left her for a younger woman.

Jimmy stood, flashed me a smile, gave Cooper a loving rough-up, then picked up his sneakers and headed for the door.

"Put them on," Betty Jean said.

"Oh, Mom, please," he said as he left.

"I'll be down in a minute," she called after him.

She stepped over to me and put her arms around my neck.

She kissed me.

I kissed her back.

My hands began to roam but she tenderly slapped them away. "I can't."

I began to nuzzle her neck. She pushed me away. "Don't make me crazy, Buddy. Deborah's having her period, and she's nuts. Jimmy has math homework. It's not that I don't want to. It's that I can't."

I understood. Betty Jean and I were an unlikely pair, but our lives had become somewhat entwined as a result of our proximity.

We were pals.

"Pals who have sex," Betty Jean once commented.

"The best kind," I had responded.

She gently touched my cheek and kissed me. Then she went downstairs.

SEVEN

"I'm taped up like some kind of mummy," Phil Dinn complained.

We were sitting in Phil's living room, me on the armchair across from the sofa on which Phil was lying, his wounded leg resting on a pair of bed pillows.

A Dodgers game was playing silently on the TV.

"Doc said I'm looking at some serious rehab. I'm lucky I don't have stairs to worry about."

Phil's was a one-story, two-bedroom ranch-style house situated on half an acre in Sherman Oaks. He and his wife, Annabel, had bought it when they first married and had raised their two boys there. It was part of a development that was constructed in the late fifties, in a neighborhood filled with similarly designed homes.

Annabel had provided me with a bottle of Heineken.

Phil was on massive doses of antibiotics and painkillers, and was restricted to ice water.

"He specify how long?"

"It'll depend on how fast I heal and get mobile again."

"Probably be easier to get back into shape if you lost a few pounds," I taunted.

"I'll take it under advisement."

"Yeah, right," I snickered.

We sat quietly watching the ball game for a while.

Then I said, "Abe fixed me up with a temporary partner."

"Oh?"

"Shelley Hartman."

"The one they call Hartman the Heartless?"

"Yeah. Her."

"For how long?"

"Until you get your sorry ass back to work. Which can't be soon enough for me. I feel awful this happened."

"It wasn't your fault, Buddy."

"Yeah, yeah. I know."

"I mean it. Don't take this out on yourself."

We turned our attention back to the game.

When I noticed Phil had dozed off, I quietly left the room, said goodnight to Annabel, and went home.

EIGHT

"So there were no repercussions?" Shelley Hartman asked, eyebrow raised.

"None," I said.

"I guess Logan's appearance didn't hurt."

"Actually, I don't think it made any difference."

A surprised smile lit up her face.

We were driving slowly west on Hollywood Boulevard.

Shelley was behind the wheel. The sky was a cloudless blue.

The cruiser's air conditioner was cranked to its highest in a fruitless attempt to combat the stifling heat of the unseasonably warm spring day.

I scanned the street in search of anything suspicious.

"And you made detective?"

"Homicide."

"Impressive."

"Thanks."

"You saw Phil?"

"Yeah."

"How's he doing?"

"Okay, I guess. He's facing a whole lot of rehab."

"So I guess you're stuck with me for a while."

"And vice versa."

We drove in silence. Shelley turned left onto La Brea Avenue and went south toward Sunset, where she turned left again and headed back in the opposite direction.

I studied her as she drove. She was my age, hard-bodied, as if once overweight but now a gym acolyte.

She had a long face, with crisply angular features. Her thick brown hair fell haphazardly to her shoulders. She was sharp-eyed, intense, and intelligent.

"Are you hearing the same stories of unrest I'm hearing?" She asked.

"You mean about the Southside standoff?"

"A lot of the locals are worried."

"Everybody is."

We were exiting the freeway at Vine Street when the radio phone barked that a domestic dispute had been reported in a low-rent apartment building located at the corner of Yucca Street and Argyle Avenue in Hollywood.

Shelley responded that she and I were close by. She activated the siren and floored the accelerator.

Minutes later, the cruiser pulled to a stop in front of the building, brakes squealing.

We leapt from the vehicle and barreled into the lobby of the shabby two-story, utilitarian edifice.

We heard screams coming from the second floor.

With weapons drawn, we raced upstairs.

There were four apartments on the floor, all of them opening onto a common landing that was accessible only by way of the main staircase. The screams were coming from apartment 2 F.

I approached the door and knocked. The screaming stopped.

"Go away," a male voice called out hoarsely from inside.

"Police officers," I called back. "Please open the door."

Silence.

"Police officers," I shouted again. "Open the door."

"I'll kill her," the male voice barked.

I looked at Shelley, who was standing behind me at the top of the staircase.

A child had begun to cry inside the apartment. "Put me down," the child screamed.

I heard the sound of a hard, angry slap.

The child screamed louder.

Then I heard a woman yell, "For chrissakes, Carl. Leave her alone."

"I'll kill her."

With this, I had heard enough.

Although no backup had yet arrived, I decided to take immediate action.

I examined the door for several moments and saw it was made of soft wood, which I deemed vulnerable. I rammed my left shoulder into it.

The hinges loosened.

Then I rammed it again, racking my shoulder in the doing, which hurt. The sound of splintering wood could be heard.

I stepped back, raised my right leg, and kicked the door in. It opened slightly and then hung askew, half on and half off its hinges.

I took a quick look inside and spied the man. A girl of about two was clutched in his arms. He ducked into an adjacent room and slammed the door behind him.

I entered the apartment and stood beside a frayed armchair, where I began rubbing my sore shoulder.

I turned and saw Shelley creep into the apartment behind me. It was postage-stamp-sized.

Stifling. Claustrophobic.

A young woman who appeared to be in her late teens was in the room. When she looked up, I noticed her bruised and bloodied face. One of her eyes was swollen shut. She appeared to have been badly beaten.

"What's that?" I said, pointing to the room into which the man and girl had disappeared.

"Bedroom."

"Tell me."

"He's got our daughter, Carla. Says he's going to kill her."

"How old?"

"Twenty-six months."

"Weapons?"

"No firearms, if that's what you're thinking."

"Why is he doing this?"

"Why? Because he's a nutcase, that's why."

"Names?"

"I'm Lorena. The asshole is Carl."

I moved away from the chair, scooted to the bedroom door, and stood beside it.

I looked back toward the front door and spotted Shelley standing inside, her service revolver in her hand.

I nodded, then called to the man in the bedroom. "Carl."

Carl didn't answer.

"I'm not here to hurt you, Carl. Please talk to me."

"I'm gonna kill her."

I could hear the child crying. "You're her father, Carl. She loves you."

"Tell that to her bitch of a mother."

I looked at Lorena.

"Ask her," Carl hollered. "Ask her how she could have done it."

"How she could have done what, Carl?"

"What she did."

I looked at Lorena again. I silently mouthed the word, "What?" Lorena looked away.

"Can we talk this out, Carl? Will you and Lorena talk this out as a family?"

"There's no talking to her."

I heard the high-pitched whine of approaching sirens. "Carl?"

Carl didn't say anything.

"Listen to me, Carl. If anything were to happen to Carla, or to Lorena, it would be awful for you. You'd never forgive yourself."

Carl remained silent.

"Don't do this, Carl. Talk to me. Let's resolve things before anyone gets hurt. Before your little girl gets hurt. Before you ruin your life."

"I don't know," Carl muttered after a while.

"I'm going to open the door," I said.

When Carl didn't respond, I reached over and turned the handle.

The door opened a crack.

Then I pushed it with my foot, opening it farther.

I could see Carl standing inside, holding the little girl in his arms.

"Put Carla down and let her come to me."

Carl glared at me.

"She's your daughter, Carl. Put her down and let her leave the room."

I saw Carl place the child on the floor. She had stopped crying. She didn't move. She looked up at him.

"Daddy," she said.

"Urge her to come out," I said.

I could hear Carl saying something to the child but couldn't make out the words.

Then she appeared in the doorway.

I reached out and took hold of her. I handed her to Lorena.

Then, without warning, I launched myself through the doorway.

Carl hadn't expected this, and he cringed at the sight of me flying toward him.

I hit him in the abdomen, knocking the wind from him, and slamming him to the floor.

Then I jumped on him, grabbed his left arm and twisted it up behind him. I pulled out zip ties from my service kit, took hold of Carl's right arm, and tied his hands together.

Carl resisted. He tried to buck me off of him, but I grabbed a fistful of his hair and yanked it upward.

Shelley Hartman appeared in the doorway, her service weapon trained on Carl.

"Stay right where you are, Carl," she hollered. "Don't move."

Carl looked at her and then slowly did as she had instructed.

I took a zip tie and wrapped it tightly around Carl's ankles.

I stared at him. He was young, baby-faced, and scared. Leaving him where he lay, I went back to the living room.

Shelley lowered her weapon and took up a post in the doorway.

Lorena was holding Carla, talking softly to her, calming her. She looked up at me.

"What happened here?" I asked.

"He went crazy."

"Why?"

"I have no idea."

I knelt down beside her. "Tell me why he went crazy."

"Ask him."

"I'm asking you."

"How in the fuck should I know?"

I was heavyhearted as I sought to bring some level of sanity to this situation. The future of these three people saddened me. They were in way over their heads. Nothing good could come of it.

The sounds of the squad car officers could be heard coming from the staircase.

"The cavalry arriveth," Shelley said. "You okay if I intercept them?"

"Yeah."

She nodded.

"Shelley?"

She turned back to me.

"Thanks."

"You did good," she said.

"You too."

She smiled, then went to greet the new arrivals.

I turned back to Lorena. "He's your husband?"

"We're not married."

"What set him off?"

"Everything sets him off. He has no job. No money. He's nobody."

"And?"

When Lorena didn't answer, I asked, "Did he have additional cause?"

She stared daggers at me. "Why would ask that? Who the fuck are you to sit in judgment of me? You don't know anything. He's a loser. We needed the money. I did what I had to do. Why don't you get the fuck out of my house?"

I looked up in time to see four police officers from the Hollywood Division storm the apartment, weapons drawn. They were accompanied by Shelley Hartman.

"It's under control," I said.

The lead officer nodded to me, and together with Shelley, they backed out of the apartment.

I returned to the bedroom.

Carl had maneuvered himself into a sitting position, in front of the bed, leaning against it.

"Violence is no way to solve problems, Carl. Especially when a child is involved. Your child. I know you think you got a raw deal, but you chose the wrong way to handle it."

"What was I supposed to do? She was turning tricks on Hollywood Boulevard, for chrissakes."

"So you thought that made it okay for you to kick the shit out of her?"

Carl sneered. Yet it appeared as if the shame of it had invaded his consciousness. An inexorable sadness hung over him.

I continued to stare at him for a while.

Then, needing to distance myself from this sorrowful scene, I left the apartment.

NINE

It was late afternoon by the time Shelley and I finished our reports and turned the matter over to the LAPD detectives.

Carl had been placed under arrest and taken away.

Social Services investigators were debating about whether or not to separate Carla from her mother.

We were grateful to be done with the case.

We climbed into the cruiser and headed back to the Hollywood station.

"How did you know?" Shelley asked.

"Know what?"

"What caused Carl to go blooey."

"There was something she wasn't telling us. Which just happened to be the defining piece of information. The elephant in the room."

"That she was hooking?"

"Exactly. I feel sorriest for the kid. What chance does she have with those two for parents? It all stinks, you know."

Shelley looked at me and nodded her agreement. "It's a cesspool out there," I said.

"And we're first in line whenever it clogs up," Shelley said.

"You noticed?"

"You thought it would be different, didn't you?"

"I hoped."

"You hoped?"

"That it might be less desolate than it is."

"What planet are you living on, Buddy?"

"I've asked myself the same question."

I find myself unexpectedly enjoying my relationship with Shelley Hartman. Her professionalism impressed me. I appreciated her forthrightness. I felt at ease with her.

"You wanna get a drink?" I asked.

"I thought you'd never ask," she joshed.

———

We were sitting at the bar in Musso and Frank, the fabled upscale tavern, a few blocks from the Hollywood station.

The dim lighting was a welcome respite from the blazing afternoon sun. The air-conditioning was a blessing. Music was playing softly in the background. I was nursing a Heineken. Shelley was sipping a gin and tonic.

"What's with this 'Hartman the Heartless?'" I asked.

"You know about that?"

"Only that it's what people call you."

Shelley took a sip of her drink. "Fucking old boys' club. It's because I broke up with Steve Marshall."

"Lieutenant Steve Marshall?"

"Yeah. Him. We were planning to get married."

I finished the beer and was considering whether or not to order a second.

"Turns out he had a secret," Shelley said. "Fortunately, I learned it in time."

"I'm not going to ask."

"Suffice it to say, it was enough to drive me away."

She downed the rest of her drink and signaled for another. I caught the bartender's eye and pointed to the empty Heineken bottle.

Shelley went on. "I broke up with him. He took it badly. Told anyone who would listen it was all my fault. That I had devastated him."

The refills arrived.

"Hartman the Heartless, he called me," Shelley lamented as she sipped her second gin and tonic. "Fucking name will follow me to my grave."

We drank in silence for a while.

Then Shelley said, "They say you played baseball."

"Some. When I was a kid. High school."

"And?"

"I don't much like to talk about it."

She nodded.

After a while, I said, "I was a fledgling shortstop. Good field, not so good hit. But I was hoping to catch on with the Dodger organization. My dad had a friend there. He arranged for me to be invited to try out for their Triple-A level affiliate in Albuquerque, so their coaching staff could have a closer look at me. I tore up my shoulder on my first day there. I was eighteen."

"What happened?"

"Third inning. Guy slides into me. Hard. Aiming to break up a double play. Upended me with his spikes."

"And?"

"I landed on my shoulder. Ripped it right out of its socket."

I took a swig of beer. "I could never make the throw again."

Sensing she had hit a nerve, she hesitated before asking, "Do you miss it?"

"Almost every day."

"What did you do?"

"Mostly I drifted. Nothing made sense. I became somewhat unhinged. Then I did a brief stretch with the Marines."

"You were a Marine?"

"Two years."

"What did you do?"

"I trained other Marines."

"In what?"

"In the fine art of being a Marine."

"And you didn't re-up?"

"No."

"Why?"

"It wasn't a business I wanted to be in any longer."

"Why not?"

"I don't know. Regimentation. Repetition. Authoritarianism."

"And that came as a surprise to you?"

"Not a surprise. An awakening. My mind hurt. So I came home. San Remo County. My father was a career police officer at the time. Preparing to run for Sheriff. He influenced me. So I took the LAPD exam and passed."

"Why LA?"

"I needed to get away from home."

"And you find being a cop different from being a Marine?"

"Not different. Better."

"How better?"

"Unpredictability. More chance for independent thought."

"And now you're going to be a homicide detective."

"Is this a great country or what?"

The front door opened and a blast of sun and heat invaded the dark and the cool of Musso's.

Officers Lonny Bentley and Bobby Harmon walked in. They spotted us.

They came over and settled in. They both ordered Miller drafts.

"Did you hear?" Bentley asked.

"Hear what?" Shelley said.

"The cops were freed. The district attorney refused to prosecute. Sheriff said they deserved what they got."

"The three guys who were murdered?"

"Yep."

"He said they deserved what they got?" Shelley asked.

"He did," Bentley said.

"But it was a cold-blooded killing."

"Not according to the DA. Or the sheriff."

"Shit's going to start flying any minute," I said.

"It already has," Harmon confirmed.

TEN

I got home in time for the evening news. There was a note from Jimmy saying he had walked and fed Cooper.

I grabbed a bottle of Bud from the fridge and settled in to watch the news.

Cooper sat beside me, also watching the news.

The acquittal of four white LAPD officers in the killing of three Black men was the lead story. It was only hours since it had been announced, yet already unrest was boiling over in South Central.

Officers of the LAPD had to be withdrawn from the area because their safety was being threatened by a growing number of irate rioters.

A white man was pulled from his vehicle by an angry mob and severely beaten. Shortly afterward, a Latino man was yanked from a truck and also beaten. Both became catalytic events, spurring an increasingly angry populace onto even greater acts of violence.

Insurgents soon began looting neighborhood stores.

Fires were set in strip malls and vacant buildings. Vast sections of South Central were ablaze. Armed thugs rampaged through the city.

I turned off the TV and cracked open another Bud. "Something, huh?" I muttered to Cooper as I took a swig.

The big bloodhound stared at me.

I contemplated the unfolding events. Tomorrow would be worse, I surmised. The violence was escalating. I feared a city-wide shutdown of businesses and services.

There were rumors of potential National Guard involvement.

I thought about Commander Jeremy Logan, who had disrupted my meeting with Internal Affairs and by so doing, effectively put an end to the investigation.

I wondered why he did it. Maybe the commander wanted me to have a clean slate when it came time for the announcement of my appointment.

I thought about Carl and Lorena. About what life would be like for the little girl. I had a sudden vision of myself as Carl. Undereducated. Unemployable. Lost. Struggling to make things right in a universe already gone desperately wrong.

These days there are too many Carls. Too many wounded and helpless people whose chances of climbing the ladder of success are mostly nonexistent.

The Carls of the world were in my thoughts. As I prepared to become a detective, I harbored the hope that during my service I might offer them some help.

The beer finally caught up with me.

I yawned.

I returned the empty bottles to the kitchen and turned off the lights.

The glow from the glimmering Hollywood night lights illuminated the bedroom.

I took off my uniform and hung it in the closet.

I washed my face and brushed my teeth. I stared at myself in the mirror. "Good night, Buddy Steel, whoever you are," I said.

Then I pushed the thoughts from my mind and laid down on the bed.

I was immediately joined there by Cooper.

Together, the two of us fell asleep.

ELEVEN

The incessant ringing of the telephone jarred me awake. It took me a moment to get my bearings.

I glanced at the bedside clock. Twelve fifteen. Just past midnight. I reached over and picked up the receiver. "Buddy Steel."

"One moment for Commander Logan," the voice on the other end of the line said.

Then I heard Logan's familiar growl. "Steel?"

"Sir."

"Sorry to wake you. I sent a car for you. It's in front of your building. I need you."

Then the phone went dead.

I leapt from the bed, suddenly alert.

I dressed hurriedly, gave Cooper a hug, closed up the apartment, and raced downstairs to the waiting vehicle.

I jumped in and the car sped away, racing toward downtown and command central.

—

Despite the lateness of the hour, Parker Center was a beehive of activity. Uniformed police officers moved through crowded hallways with determination and purpose. Telephones rang ceaselessly. Reporters roamed the building in search of exclusive tidbits.

I stood before the desk sergeant, waiting until the harried policeman finished a phone call and looked up at me.

"Buddy Steel for Commander Logan."

"Room 244," the officer said, returning to the phones.

I found Logan's suite. Three police officers sat at separate desks in the anteroom, each on the phone. One looked up at me.

"Detective Steel?" She asked.

"Officer Steel," I said, by way of correction.

The policewoman nodded. "Commander L is in Chief MacLeod's office," she said. "They're waiting for you. Top floor. Executive suite."

"Thank you."

"You'll need this."

She handed me a floor pass. I took it and headed for the bank of elevators, one of which whisked me into the stratosphere.

I handed the pass to the sergeant on duty, who then led me to Chief Andrew MacLeod's office, which offered a majestic view of Los Angeles, ranging from the nearby Music Center all the way to the ocean.

Logan sat across the desk from the chief, a weathered veteran of some forty-plus years of service.

MacLeod's tired gaze reflected the stress and tension brought upon him by the onset of the riots.

The two officers stood to greet me. We all shook hands, and Chief MacLeod offered coffee, which I greatly appreciated.

"We've got ourselves a situation," Logan said.

I took a sip of coffee and felt the first warm jolt of caffeine as it coursed its way through my system.

"A question," Chief MacLeod said as he started pacing around the office. "Are you aware of the recent rise in methamphetamine-related gang activity in Los Angeles County?"

"Yes, sir. I am."

"So you know this drug business is on track to achieve epidemic proportions, particularly here in the city?"

"Yes, sir, I do."

"For a number of weeks now," MacLeod said, "we've been hearing rumors of an imminent delivery of what is being termed as vast quantities of a very sophisticated crystal meth. Compliments of the Magdalena cartel in northern Mexico, and Los Pacos, their friends here in South Central.

"It makes sense, because the streets have gone dry, and we're now detecting a heightened level of gang activity that we believe is anticipatory of a major drug drop. We've been working with the federal authorities in a collective effort to seize this shipment, which is expected to arrive in Los Angeles next week."

The chief stopped pacing and focused his attention on me. "Yesterday changed all that. These damn riots have created a great deal of havoc. Key to our efforts, one of our undercover agents, posing as a wealthy buyer, was in contact with a ranking member of Los Pacos. Our agent attended a meeting with this person on Tuesday. Following which he disappeared.

"This evening he turned up in South Central. His severed head was found several yards from his body."

Both men looked at me.

"We want you to take his place," MacLeod said.

TWELVE

Chief Andrew MacLeod planted himself in front of me. "We have to get inside again," he said. "We need to know why our operative was dispatched. And more importantly, we have to learn whether our mission has been compromised. We're looking to you to determine this, Buddy."

Something about this scenario raised my hackles. It didn't feel right. I couldn't put my finger on it, but the chief's story somehow felt incomplete. Uncertain.

I looked at MacLeod. "What is it you're not telling me?"

"Excuse me?"

"What's missing?"

"Why would you ask that?"

"Because I'm an unlikely choice."

"Not to us," Logan said.

"I've never worked undercover before."

"We believe that to be an asset."

"Why?"

"None of these narco-traffickers know you. You're a virgin. You're above suspicion."

"We have great faith in you, Steel," MacLeod said. "Time isn't in our favor. We need to act now. Despite your reservations, we all feel you're the best man for the job. Will you do it?"

I was torn between latching on to the opportunity I was being offered or passing on it and losing the confidence and support of both Chief MacLeod, and more importantly, Commander Logan.

I shouldn't have been tendered this furball. I fretted over what made them choose me until finally, I threw in the towel.

I mean, what the hell. You only live once.

"Bring it on," I said to Chief MacLeod.

———

Logan and I left the chief's office, and headed downstairs, where we were joined by Murray Goodman, Logan's deputy, and the project manager for "Operation Los Pacos," as it had come to be known.

Deputy Captain Goodman, a widely experienced law enforcement official in his early forties, was already engaged in a struggle to maintain his youthful appearance. A struggle he was losing.

His once-ample mane had been reduced to a handful of isolated strands that he combed flatly across the top of his head.

He had developed a pair of deeply etched jowls that robbed his face of any of its remaining youthfulness.

His large veiny nose contributed to his dissipated appearance.

Desk work had brought with it a thickening middle and an even thicker behind.

Some in the department believed it had also endowed him with an exasperatingly thicker head.

I had known Murray Goodman for some time and wasn't his biggest fan. I considered him supercilious and vain, and while we both made an effort toward cordiality, it was a fragile bond we hung onto precipitously, one constantly in danger of collapsing.

Logan handed me over to Goodman and once again turned his attention to the rapidly escalating civilian unrest in South Central that was gaining steam, with mobs of rioters currently heading east toward Koreatown.

"Coffee?" Goodman asked as we settled into his small office adjacent to Logan's.

"Please," I said.

Goodman pressed the intercom button on his desk phone and requested two cups.

He picked up a yellow legal pad and a pen, swung his heavy legs onto his desk and leaned back in his desk chair. "Where should we start?" he said.

"First tell me about Phyllis and the kids," I queried in an effort to shore up our shaky underpinnings.

"Toledo."

"Ohio?"

"Living with her parents."

"Living with them?"

"She left one day in the middle of my shift. No warning."

"Did she say why?"

"She told me I was married to the job. That she had become an accessory."

"You talking to anyone?"

"You mean like a shrink?"

"Yes."

"I don't believe in shrinks."

"How do you deal with the anger?"

"I don't know, Buddy. I guess I keep it bottled up."

"Can't be good for you, Murray."

"How 'bout I don't want to talk about it. Okay, Buddy?"

The moment was rescued when the door to the office opened and a middle-aged officer entered, carrying a tray containing a coffeepot, two cups, and sundry accoutrements.

He set down the tray, poured the coffee, nodded to Goodman, then left the room.

"The downed officer was Nicholas Morgan," Goodman said, changing the subject. "We had crafted his identity as a well-to-do financial manager named Ryan Scott, a recreational meth user, a moderate-sized buyer for a well-to-do group of his clients.

"After poking around the club scene for a while, Nick made contact with the man we believe to be the prime mover of product for Los Pacos, a strange bird called Freddy Sunday, who arranged for Nick to make a few minor buys.

"When rumors began flying about the size and quality of the upcoming drop, Nick told Sunday he wanted to make a bigger score. He said he was prepared to spend up to a hundred thousand dollars."

"And?"

"It seemed to go well. At least that's what Nick thought."

"And?"

"He told us Freddy Sunday had requested a follow-up meeting at some downtown club. Nick went to the meeting. Then he vanished."

"What do you think happened?"

"We don't really know," Goodman said. "He was found in South Central, but forensics thinks he died elsewhere and his body was dumped there."

"Why?"

"To throw us off track."

"Why do you think he was killed?"

"That's the sixty-four-million-dollar question, isn't it?"

"What can you tell me about Freddy Sunday?"

"His real name is Federico Domingo and he's close to Francisco Reyes, the head of operations for the Pacos."

"Is there any background material?"

Goodman handed me a thickly packed file folder. "Whatever we have is in there."

"What do I need to know about Nicholas Morgan?"

"It's in there. There's also the Beverly Hills house in which we set him up. Robert Mitchum's old house, actually."

"I'll want to have a look at it."

Goodman handed me a set of keys. "It's under surveillance," he said. "Just in case."

"In case what?"

"In case anyone starts nosing around it."

"What about backup?"

"Only if you want it."

"I want it."

"Do you have someone in mind?"

"I have a new partner."

"Hartman the Heartless?"

I flashed him a cheerless glance. "Shelley Hartman."

"You want to work with her?"

"Yes."

"Okay."

I sat silently for a while, thumbing idly through the file. "There is one other thing."

"What?"

"What aren't you telling me, Murray?"

After a few moments, Goodman said, "We also have another someone on the inside."

"Inside where?"

"Inside the Paco hierarchy."

"How far inside?"

"Very significantly inside."

After a few moments, Goodman added, "It's someone you know."

"You've got an inside operative whom I know?"

"Yes."

"Who?"

Goodman didn't respond.

"Who is it, Murray?"

"Kara Machado."

"Kara?"

"Yes."

"Really?"

"Yeah," Goodman said.

"Does she know about me?"

"No."

"She has no idea of this new assignment?"

"None."

"I can't do it, Murray. She'll freak the moment she sees me."

"Not a chance. She's a highly trained operative, Buddy. One of our best. We're currently in the dark regarding whether or not she, too, has been compromised. If so, she's living under a death threat. The fact she knows you is the reason you were selected."

"So I was right."

"Right about what?"

"There was a withhold. I don't like this one bit, Murray."

"You know what, Buddy?" Goodman said. "Get over it."

THIRTEEN

Often, when I felt certain I was done with her, Kara Machado reclaimed my thoughts.

I met her on my first day at the academy. She was in all of my classes. I couldn't take my eyes off her.

Chestnut-brown hair framed her angular face in a short, frenetic confusion of unruly spikes and cowlicks. She was lithe and sensual. Kinetic. Dynamic. Exceptionally smart and street savvy. Her deep amber eyes burned with a fiery intensity.

I pursued her.

She resisted.

I asked questions.

She gave one-word answers.

She was distant and aloof.

But I was persistent. Finally she softened. Mostly because I made her laugh.

One night she agreed to have dinner with me.

That was the beginning.

For a while we were on fire. She was sexually aggressive and bold. I had never been with anyone like her. I was bewitched.

Her career sights were set on the stars. She was an ardent

student. Her commitment to academic excellence began to infuse me with a similar passion to become better, to raise my standards.

I fell hopelessly in love with her.

Then, without warning, everything changed.

Kara had a great many things to prove, and she soon realized that tying herself to one man was anathema to her plan. She began to withdraw. She grew distant. Finally, she put an end to it.

Although classes at the academy still brought us together, she kept her distance.

Then the semester was over, and she vanished from my life.

I had terrible difficulty coming to grips with what happened. I blamed myself. I became moody. I suffered melancholia. On more than one occasion, I drank too much.

Now this.

"Just when I thought I was out," to quote Michael Corleone, "She pulls me back in."

———

As feared, rioting erupted in South Central.

By midafternoon, things had worsened. Looting was rampant and having learned of an absence of a significant police presence in Koreatown of all places, the rioters flocked there in droves.

Many Korean store owners, on alert since the verdict was announced, took up residence in their places of business, armed and dangerous.

Gun battles broke out, some even televised. Numbers of people were wounded.

Widespread arson caused parts of the area to become infernos. Firefighters were forced to operate under police protection.

The governor called out the California National Guard.

The president appeared on TV, pleading for calm.

A dusk-to-dawn curfew went into effect.

Getting into and out of South Central, for the time being at least, was near impossible.

"So, who's Kara Machado?" Shelley asked.

She was driving a late-model black Mercedes sedan, courtesy of the LAPD motor pool, heading west toward Beverly Hills.

I sat beside her.

"We were at the academy together."

"So?"

"So...what?"

"Don't go all silent on me, Buddy. I'm your partner, remember?"

"Temp partner."

"Partner just the same."

After a while I said, "We were very close."

"You and Kara."

"Yes."

"How close?"

"Close. Let's just say we were together."

"You mean you were a couple?"

"Not exactly a couple."

"Why is this so difficult?" Shelley muttered.

"Why don't we just leave it at we were together?"

Neither of us spoke for a while.

It felt odd to be talking about Kara. I had wrestled with my thoughts of her. Now, unexpectedly, those thoughts and the attendant hurt they carried with them flooded over me.

Shelley persisted. "So, what happened?"

I involuntarily sighed. "She dumped me. It took a while to get over her."

"How long?"

"Long."

After letting that settle in, Shelley asked, "When did you see her last?"

"Two years ago."

"And she's the inside plant?"

"Yes."

"And there's a chance she may have been compromised?"

"That's what Goodman implied."

"And she has no idea you've been conscripted?"

"None."

"So, what could go wrong?"

———

The Mercedes reached Beverly Hills, and Shelley turned right onto Alta Drive, heading up the hill.

Spacious, multimillion-dollar homes were shielded from view by pine, live oak, maple, and juniper trees. Ferns, yucca, creeping vines, and wild grape bushes, some surpassing ten feet in height, grew in abundance.

The cool, spring air was ripe with the fragrance of blooming orange, sage, and evening primrose. It was a far cry from the densely packed streets of most of Los Angeles County.

The Mitchum estate was on the left.

As Shelley made the turn, she noticed the patrol car parked across the street. She waved to the officers inside and headed up the winding driveway. Once at the intercom box in front of a large iron gate, she punched in four numbers. The gate swung open.

The paved driveway wound its way through a thicket of privet hedges, and past a three-hole putting green situated directly across the driveway from the majestic front door of the wood-and-glass two-story manse.

She pulled to a stop and we got out of the car.

We stood staring at the house.

"Robert Mitchum?" she asked.

"That's what Murray said."

"How ironic."

"Ironic?"

"He was the original Hollywood druggie. Even did some jail time."

"That is ironic."

"You want to go inside?" she asked.

"Probably better than standing here gaping."

The house was surprisingly cool and dark.

The entranceway opened onto an ornately designed foyer that fronted a wall-sized picture window and a grand staircase.

We began nosing around.

Downstairs we discovered a ballroom-sized living room, an ample den, plus a vast dining room containing a cherrywood table with twelve matching chairs.

The oversized kitchen featured restaurant-quality appliances, as well as a breakfast nook that seated eight.

Behind the kitchen, we found a suite of rooms that I took to be maids' quarters.

Upstairs consisted of four bedrooms, all of them suites, each containing a full bath and separate sitting area.

The largest bedroom was three times the size of my entire Hollywood apartment.

We wound up back in the kitchen.

"You think there's anything to drink around here?" Shelley asked.

I looked inside the KitchenAid refrigerator and found it stocked with juices and sodas, beers, and wines.

"So much for Nicholas Morgan's frugality," Shelley said.

"I wonder what his expense account looked like," I added.

"Is there a Coke?"

I grabbed her one and took a Hires root beer for myself. We sat at the kitchen table.

"There's enough room here to house the entire U.S. Navy," Shelley said.

"Probably take us a while to sift through it all."

"We got something better to do?"

FOURTEEN

I had just begun my examination of Nick Morgan's bedroom when the gate intercom sounded.

After a frantic search for the control box, I found it and pressed intercom.

"Speak," I said.

"Byron Prescott," came the muted response. I didn't say anything.

"*The* Byron Prescott."

Again I didn't say anything.

"Open the fucking gate, Buddy, or I'll climb over it and brain you," Prescott said.

"Why didn't you say so?"

I punched in the code that activated the gate.

Shelley and I reached the door in time to see a late-model Chevy Impala pull up in front of the house.

The man who stepped out resembled a thirtysomething junior executive, nattily dressed in a navy blazer worn over a powder-blue shirt and sharply pressed khaki trousers. His red bow tie was sprinkled with white polka dots. An ear-to-ear grin was plastered on his face.

"Buddy Steel," he said.

"Byron Prescott," I said. "I thought you had been drummed out of the department years ago."

"You wish."

We embraced, each of us slapping the other heartily on the back. We had attended the academy together and had been close friends. After graduation, however, we had drifted apart.

"Shelley Hartman," I said by way of introduction.

"Hartman the..." Byron began.

"Go ahead," Shelley hissed, "say it. I dare you."

"How do you do, Shelley Hartman?"

She glared at him.

He grinned.

"Nice house," he said. "Amazing the riffraff they allow in it, though."

"Riffraff?" I goaded.

"If the shoe fits," Byron said.

We went inside. He gazed at the daunting entrance foyer. "They say that Robert Mitchum once lived here."

"You want to tell me why you're here, Byron?"

"Special Ops. Tactical forces. Here to administer an intro-ductory lesson titled *How Not to Get Killed by a Drug Cartel.*"

"Special Ops?"

"Since ninety-nine."

Shelley suggested we all sit in the den.

After she and I had fetched some drinks, we settled into the comfortable den that featured rich mahogany bookcases on all four walls, each sporting a wide range of eclectic titles.

Dormer-style windows were sculpted into two of the book-cases, both throwing slashes of light across the highly polished parqueted floor.

Plushly upholstered sofas and chairs formed a conversation pit in the center of the room.

I switched on a pair of retro-style floor lamps that provided a soft, comforting glow. We sat across from each other.

"How long since you've seen her?" Byron asked.

"Two years, more or less."

"And?"

"Let's drop it, shall we?"

"You're not still..."

"Let's just say it was a difficult hill to climb."

"And?"

"Goodman told me she's the reason I was chosen."

"Sweet."

"Exactly."

Byron cleared his throat and began in earnest. "Los Pacos," he said. "In English: The Pacos."

"This guy sure knows his stuff," I murmured to Shelley out of the side of my mouth.

Byron ignored me.

"Their origins were in Cartagena, Colombia. In the late eighties. They were part of a splinter group that broke away from the Cali cartel, which pretty much ran things down there.

"At first the group was small potatoes, and the cartel left them alone. But after a while, it gained enough steam to attract attention and earn them a warning that came in the form of the beheading of Ernesto Gonzalez, the group's leader.

"That was when the cousins Reyes, Paco José and Paco Luis, decided to emigrate to Mexico, where opportunities appeared to abound and personal safety wasn't an issue.

"They resettled on the Gulf of California, in the northern coastal village of Puerto Peñasco in the Sonoran province, where they had family.

"There they enlisted the services of their Sonoran-born cousin, also named Paco. So now they were three, and they set out to rule the world. Or at the very least, northern Mexico.

"They conducted a number of raids on plush ranchos, plundering and killing as they saw fit. Soon they had gathered an ample amount of capital and they proceeded to put it to work for them."

Byron pulled a small photo album from his pocket and showed it to Shelley and me. He pointed to candid photos taken of each of the founding Pacos.

"First thing they did was create a security force. Or should I say a small army, numbers of whom were moonlighting, holding on to their day jobs as either police officers or soldiers, all the while fattening their purses with the Pacos's *dinero*.

"In short order, Los Pacos seized control of the Magdalenas, a small, family-run drug operation, also Sonora-based. They systematically wiped out the Magdalenas. Killed every one of them, many brutally.

"The Pacos had delivered their intended message. They became universally feared. Their rule went unchallenged. They began farming the land they had confiscated. They raised but a single crop."

"Peaches?" I asked.

Byron snickered. "High-quality marijuana. And of course, they flourished."

"Is that the end of the story?"

"Would that it were. There was never enough *dinero* to satisfy Los Pacos. They introduced their product into the American marketplace, insinuating it into key cities such as Los Angeles, Tucson, and Houston. Weed was the crop on which they founded their empire, but crystal meth became the jewel in their crown. Today's drug of choice," Byron said.

"You mentioned Los Angeles," I said.

"I did. Los Pacos are a major force in Los Angeles. Francisco Reyes is The Man. And ironically, no one has ever heard of him.

"Number one son of Paco José Reyes. Twenty-nine years old. Looks and acts like a movie star. And get this, he's a Harvard graduate.

"Since taking charge, he's led the enterprise in an entirely different direction. He legitimized it. He created a whole new image for the Pacos. And more to the point, he's taken their narcotics operations so deeply underground that they can barely be located.

"He runs things from an office tower in Century City. He lives in a gated Malibu enclave. His comings and goings are a closely held secret. He's always surrounded by a cadre of bodyguards."

Byron flipped the pages in his photo album until he found the one of Francisco Reyes, his graduation photo as it appeared in the Harvard yearbook.

"*El Jefe*, himself," he said. "Señor Francisco Gilberto Alcala Moreno y Reyes."

"Wow," Shelley said. "All those names and a hunk too."

"Don't be fooled by his looks," Byron said. "He's lethal."

"An educated drug lord," I said. "How does he get away with it?"

"He's untouchable. Lawyers, lawyers, and more lawyers. Oh, and did I mention lawyers?"

"Is this paradise or what?" I said. "How do *los tres* regard their legitimization?"

"*Los tres* have morphed into *el uno*. Paco Luis quit the business, married an Australian, and moved to the outback. Cousin Paco died. Only Francisco's father, Paco José, is still around, and rumor has it he's unwell."

"So Francisco is really the *jefe*?"

"I believe he'd rather be thought of as the CEO," Byron said.

"He considers himself a modern-day businessman and behaves accordingly."

"What does he do?"

"What do you mean?"

"You know, what does he do for fun? How does he unwind?"

"As you might expect of a CEO. He plays a little golf. Sees a few movies. Oh, and he likes to dine out," Byron said.

"Married?"

"Not that we know of. But he does have a live-in companion."

"Kara?" I asked.

"Kara," Byron confirmed.

FIFTEEN

I turned the big Mercedes sedan onto Avenue of the Stars in Century City and cruised slowly in search of number 2050.

"Did you know that Kara lives with him?" Shelley asked.

"No."

"This whole thing begins to smell worse and worse," she said.

"It's like they set me up."

"Yeah, but for what?"

I spotted number 2050 and pulled up in front. It was a towering building, all steel and glass, tall even by Century City standards. It had been built on the site of what had once been the main gate to the 20th Century-Fox Studios back in the day when it was owned by its founder, William Fox.

Shelley got out and headed for the building.

I remained in the Mercedes with the motor idling and the air conditioner chilling.

My thoughts drifted to Kara and the night she left.

For a lengthy spell afterward, our final conversation kept insinuating itself into my mind, a self-torment I had come to believe was over but now returned with a vengeance.

"Why, Kara?" I kept asking her.

"I don't know, Buddy. I'm not ready for this."

"For what?"

"This kind of commitment. I'm not there."

"You'll get there."

"I won't."

"Give it a little more time."

"You're too hungry, Buddy."

"What hungry? I love you, Kara."

"You love me too much."

"That's bullshit, and you know it."

"I'm not going to argue with you. This is way too intense for me. I can't handle it. I can't handle you. I'm sorry. I just can't."

She hurriedly gathered whatever belongings she had and threw them into her duffel.

Then she was gone, leaving me confused and desolate.

Ironic, I mused, given my now-infamous resistance to emotional commitment. Likely they're connected.

My reverie was broken by Shelley Hartman's return.

She climbed into the Mercedes with a glum look on her face.

"Penthouse," she said. "Private elevator. When I pressed the button for the elevator, two security guards appeared."

"Let me guess. They wouldn't admit you."

"I wasn't on the list. I tried to talk my way in, but no soap. They actually became testy."

"Testy?"

"They were impertinent and impatient. They escorted me out of the building."

"In Century City?"

"Hard to believe, isn't it?"

"Seems as if Reyes Enterprises might have something to hide."

"It does, doesn't it?"

I made a U-turn on Olympic Boulevard and headed west toward Malibu.

"Where to now?" Shelley inquired.

"Let's go see where the son of a bitch lives."

———

The Reyes compound sat high on a bluff overlooking the ocean and was surrounded by a dense forest of maple, walnut, and Heritage oak trees that not only provided massive amounts of shade, but also shielded the compound from inquisitive eyes.

The main entrance was located on Pacific Coast Highway. It was gated, and a small guardhouse was the only structure visible from the road.

A tough-looking hombre sat on a bench in front of it, smoking. A rifle could be seen at his feet.

I drove past it.

"Geoffrey's?" I asked Shelley.

"That's the one," she answered.

During our ride west, Shelley had phoned each of the notable restaurants in the Malibu area, seeking confirmation of a Reyes reservation for that evening.

Responding to her authoritative manner, the young man who answered the phone at Geoffrey's, the legendary Malibu oceanfront eatery, confirmed that an F. Reyes had booked a table for two at eight that evening.

At a quarter to eight, I was seated alone at Geoffrey's bar, nursing a gin and tonic.

At a few minutes past eight, the Reyes party entered the restaurant, preceded by a pair of security guards, both wearing black suits, white shirts, and gray ties.

Before they would allow Reyes to enter, the guards scanned

the room, searching for anyone or anything that might appear suspicious.

One of the men's gaze landed on me. I returned it indifferently.

After several moments, seemingly satisfied that no threat to the well-being of their charges would be posed at Geoffrey's, the guards allowed Reyes and his companion to be ushered inside.

I watched out of the corner of my eye as the couple crossed in front of me, following the maître d' to their assigned table.

Francisco was even more attractive than his photo had led me to believe. He was indeed movie-star handsome, dressed casually in a navy blue Ralph Lauren suit, his cream-colored shirt open at the neck.

His companion was equally charismatic, wearing a tight-fitting black dress that called attention to her lissome figure. Chestnut brown hair flowed sensuously over her bare shoulders. She was deeply tanned, and her skin glistened.

Francisco held the chair for her as she sat. Her amber eyes scanned the room. They swept past me without so much as a glimmer of recognition.

Then, when Francisco turned his back to her and headed for his own chair, her eyes returned to mine and held them for a moment.

She silently mouthed the words, "Help me."

SIXTEEN

Shelley and I assiduously avoided freeway closures, curfew regulations, and the ongoing skirmishes between rioters and police as we made our way downtown to Parker Center.

The nature of a major city in total shutdown mode is surreal. Streets are devoid of traffic. Armed soldiers intercept people at random. Blockades are placed at key intersections, and drivers whose vehicles somehow manage to be on the road are subject to interrogation, inspection, and possible imprisonment.

Major Hollywood thoroughfares were starkly illuminated by hastily erected klieg lights, making them appear as if they were being featured in a movie, one devoid of any visible actors.

It also seemed as if an all-powerful sound engineer had pulled the ultimate plug, thereby plunging the city into a ghostly silence.

We were awaiting a hastily arranged audience with Commander Logan and Murray Goodman.

We caught a glimpse of Byron Prescott scurrying through the crowded hallways of the command center and assumed he would also be joining us.

The door to Logan's office opened, and the garrulous official appeared, signaling for us to enter.

Goodman and Prescott suddenly showed up, and they, too, stepped into the office.

"Good evening," Logan said in his usual growl. "Or is it good morning? I can't tell the difference any longer. I'm not even certain what day it is."

He went directly to the subject at hand. "How did she seem to you?" he asked me.

"Hard to say. She displayed no visible sign of emotion. She mouthed the words 'Help me' when Reyes had his back to her."

"It's appropriate, then, for us to assume she's experiencing some form of distress."

"Only if we interpret the words '*Help me*' as a sign of distress."

"Let's keep the sarcasm to a minimum, can we please, Buddy?" Murray Goodman interjected.

"The question is what do we do next?" Byron asked.

"I propose we go forward as planned," Goodman responded.

"Meaning?"

"We need to learn if and when the meth drop is going to take place. The bust is our priority."

"More so than getting our operative out of harm's way?"

"I believe so, yes," Goodman said. "By tomorrow, with the National Guard in place, it's likely we'll have more of a lid on the civil unrest. There might even be some semblance of order. I'm guessing the junkies will crawl out of hiding, and the Pacos will show up to service them. I propose Buddy goes ahead with his investigation as planned."

"You're suggesting that before the riots are totally quelled, I should brave a foray into a curfewed area to learn when a narcotics drop might take place?"

"That's how we originally planned it."

"But you planned it before the rioting began."

"Yes."

"And you want to stick to that plan?"

"Yes."

"You're kidding, right?"

"I don't kid," Goodman sneered imperiously.

I had little patience for Goodman's jabbering. I found myself in disagreement with him more often than not.

"What planet do you live on, Murray?" I said. "No one's going to be making drug deals. They're firing real bullets out there."

"I realize things are out of the ordinary."

"An appearance by Darth Vader would be out of the ordinary. What you're proposing is lunacy."

"If I'm not mistaken, I believe I asked you to dial down the sarcasm."

When he realized my temperature was rising, Byron asked me, "What is it you would propose?"

"That we focus our attention on rescuing Kara."

"And just how do you suggest we do that?" Byron asked.

"We snatch her. In a restaurant. In her car. From Santa's lap, if we have to. Anywhere she might be."

"Impossible," Goodman said.

"Impossible?"

"This is the United States of America. We don't just go around snatching citizens."

"We're talking about a fellow police officer in distress, not some random citizen."

"And how would we receive authorization for such an undertaking?"

"Authorization?"

"That's right."

"This would be a legitimate police action. No authorization is necessary."

"Somebody has to approve it," Goodman said.

I turned to Commander Logan. "Will you approve it?"

Before he could speak, Goodman once again chimed in.

"Don't put the commander on the spot," he said. "Obviously he disagrees with you."

"Kara Machado is one of your detectives, isn't she?" I asked Logan.

Logan nodded.

"In the face of what we've already learned, are you saying you'd be willing to simply let her dangle?"

"He didn't say that," Goodman contested.

"I submit it's our duty to make every possible effort to rescue her. Whether it's in your playbook or not, Murray."

"We disagree on that, Buddy."

"What disagree? You're dead fucking wrong."

"Is this sudden interest of yours professional or personal?"

"Low blow, Murray. I only wish it was your sorry ass hanging out there. I bet you'd be singing an entirely different song were that the case."

"That's what you say."

"All right, all right," Logan said. "That's enough. Officer Steel makes a compelling argument."

He turned to Deputy Goodman. "I want you to prepare a report proposing ways in which we might extricate Kara Machado."

Goodman stood. "Surely you don't mean to scotch our plan, do you, sir?"

"Before we proceed, I want to consider some alternative proposals. Steel's right. We have some time. Let's use it to our advantage."

"But, sir..."

"This meeting's over," Logan said. "Everybody out."

One by one, the participants filed out of the office, no one daring to make eye contact with any of the others. Shelley and

I made our way to the bank of elevators. Goodman hurried to catch up.

"One moment, Buddy."

"One moment for what? More of your bullshit? You were out of line in there, Murray. It's only on the strength of our past relationship that I don't pick you up and throw you against the wall."

"I'm the commander's deputy, Buddy. Don't fuck with me. Don't face me in front of my boss. I have a job to do."

"Then do it. But do it right. Do it in a way that shows at least a modicum of respect for a fellow officer in distress."

"Don't lecture me, Buddy."

"I wouldn't lower myself."

The elevator doors opened. Shelley and I got in.

Neither of us looked at Goodman as the doors were closing.

SEVENTEEN

We drove in silence. Shelley was behind the wheel.

"I smell a rat," she said after a while.

"That obvious, huh?"

"Amazing Logan keeps him around. He sure seems like a guy who's primarily out to protect his own skin."

"He wasn't always that way."

"I think you should play his game," Shelley said, glancing at me.

"Meaning?"

"If it were me, I'd jettison Goodman's plan."

"In favor of?"

"That's up to you, Buddy. I'm seeing a great deal of chaos now. The riots have changed things. You might have the opportunity to take things into your own hands."

I thought about that for a while.

"I've been thinking the same thing," I said.

"Meaning?"

"I have a Plan B in mind. The one where I get to do things my way. The 'no rules' way. The 'abide the events' way. The one where I get Kara out of there any way I can."

"And you're going to tell that to Logan?"

"I am."

"And if he disagrees?"

"He won't disagree."

"Even if it blows the drug deal?"

"Nothing's gonna blow the drug deal. It might have to be delayed, but Francisco has too much at stake to blow it. Besides, he's far too arrogant. He perceives himself as omnipotent."

"And you're going to prove otherwise?"

"Look at it this way, Shelley. The riots have thrown a huge monkey wrench into everything. You see how distracted Logan is. How exhausted. Los Pacos have been bumped several notches lower on the department's priority list. Everyone's attentions are focused elsewhere."

"Which allows Logan a pathway to giving you free rein to work in and around the riots," Shelley said.

"Yes."

"And Goodman?"

"Goodman's irrelevant. He's a theorist. And it's clear that Logan is already questioning his theories. We're his only viable option."

"Because?"

"Because he knows I'll stop at nothing to free her. And he also knows I'm crazy enough to pull it off."

———

I was once again standing in front of Jeremy Logan's desk. Dawn had not yet broken.

Logan pointed to the chair across from him. After such a long night, he seemed tired and withdrawn. None too pleased to see me again.

"What now?" the commander asked.

I made my case.

"I'm your best option," I said in conclusion.

"Hi yo, Silver," Logan chided. "Do you really believe I'd team up with The Lone Ranger?"

"You've got nobody better to team up with."

"You wouldn't stand a chance."

"Forgive my impudence, sir, but we're already out of time. Morgan's dead. The drug drop is in jeopardy. And Kara's in obvious danger. They likely believe she's their enemy, and won't be timid about exacting retribution. For all we know, she could already be dead."

Logan sighed heavily.

"There's no one but my team and me who can save her. Especially with these riots distracting everyone."

I watched as Logan pondered his options. "What would you need?" he said at last.

"The widest possible berth."

"Meaning?"

"I'll need to do it my way. And with the resources to do it properly."

"Okay."

"I need Shelley Hartman with me. She's tough as nails. And Byron Prescott too. He's an excellent strategist."

"And that's it?"

"Almost."

"What else?"

"Detective First Class status."

"Because?"

"It will give me greater authority."

Logan thought about it for a while. Then he said, "All right."

"So, it's a deal?"

The commander stood wearily. The riots had taken their toll on him. He was exhausted.

"Let me tell you something, Buddy," he said. "A few words of wisdom from an old man. You're one of the bright lights around here. You have initiative, as well as an innate understanding of the way things really are. You're fearless. And you exhibit remarkable ingenuity.

"I like you. I see much of the younger me in you. Much of the me that wasn't yet tempered or hardened by the weight of experience.

"What happens next will most likely be a defining moment for you. If you succeed, you'll no doubt earn recognition and reward. If you fail, it will stay with you for the rest of your life.

"Don't underestimate these Pacos. The odds are heavily in their favor. Trust your instincts and act accordingly. As Robert Kennedy was fond of saying, 'Do your best and then to hell with it.'"

"Meaning?"

"Don't fuck up."

———

When I finally got home, the dark of night was just giving way to a hazy morning glow.

Low clouds hung heavily in the orange sky, carrying with them the threat of rain and the promise of heat and humidity. A gentle wind carried the smell of smoke with it.

I spotted Jimmy's note, saying he had fed and walked Cooper.

I washed my face, brushed my teeth, and climbed into bed, noticing at last that Betty Jean was stirring beside me.

"Tough night?" she asked with a yawn.

"How long have you been here?"

"I came up after the kids went to bed. What time is it?"

"Five thirty."

"How bad?"

"The rioting?"

"Yes."

"Pretty bad."

"Here, too?"

"Not in Hollywood. There's too big a police presence on the streets."

"So we'll be safe?"

"Yes."

Betty Jean yawned again and stretched. A lascivious look lit up her face. "We have about an hour."

She snuggled up beside me. "Unless you're too tired, that is."

"An hour?"

"Yes."

"Not enough time."

"Prove it."

I pulled her to me and gently kissed her. Then I kissed her with more urgency.

She tossed off the blankets, revealing her nakedness. "I always come prepared," she chided.

After that we didn't speak for a while.

EIGHTEEN

The riots had put a real crimp in Francisco Reyes's plans. Just when things were going so well for both him and Freddy.

It now appeared likely the meth drop would have to be postponed, the result of the breakout of the riots. It was then that Freddy became suspicious of the buyer called Ryan Scott.

Scott, a newly acquired customer, had been introduced to Freddy as a high-profile financial adviser. He came complete with all of the appropriate bona fides. He had an office in Beverly Hills, a clientele that allegedly numbered among it a handful of the town's brightest and richest, and he was a fixture in the LA club scene.

Freddy was an upscale urban gadfly who moved regularly in the circles of the elite, those who dabbled in the underground drug culture and habituated the socially promiscuous club scene.

He had become a denizen of the fashion universe, having turned himself into a postmodern clotheshorse by outfitting himself in the new wave, trendy designs of the yet to be discovered mode-setters such as John Galliano, Romeo Gigli, and Issey Miyake.

His vanity was legion, and he never left home without having been freshly coiffed and expertly made-up. He caused a stir wherever he went.

It had been his and Francisco's idea to insinuate Freddy into the LA social scene and to use his status there as a means of supplying high-end Paco product to its cash-rich habitués.

Although many knew of Freddy, only the superrich were allowed access to him and his services. He never handled the product nor the cash himself, but he masterminded the deals and then steered the buyers to those who did.

Freddy had proved himself invaluable to Reyes Enterprises. He was the earner supreme, providing a revenue flow that was unmatched by any other sales operative.

Federico Domingo had grown up in Puerto Peñasco. His father was the Sonoran accountant for Los Tres Pacos and as such, was close to the Reyes family. It was through him that Freddy met Francisco.

They became fast friends. They were inseparable. The two boys went through middle and high school together, and when Francisco went to Harvard, Freddy enrolled in Boston's Emerson College to be near him.

When Francisco chose the family business, Freddy joined him.

They had long dreamed of living in Los Angeles and becoming Hollywood heavyweights. They envisioned a time when their involvement in the narcotics trade would be phased out and they would instead become culture kings, with interests not only in film and television, but in fashion, nightclubs, and music as well.

Under Francisco's stewardship, they were already taking giant steps in that direction.

While Francisco was conservative and private, Freddy was garish and public. He wasn't exactly handsome, but he was extremely charismatic, lean, and seductive. He was a magnet for the rich and beautiful. He was androgynously sensual, and speculation about his sexual appetites ran rampant.

But Freddy also frequented the dark side. He was known to have a short fuse and a penchant for violence. In times of duress, he was invariably Francisco's go-to person, and was regularly called upon to resolve any unpleasantness that threatened the security of Reyes Enterprises. It was widely understood that Freddy would stop at nothing to protect the Reyeses' interests.

Frankie and Freddy breakfasted together every morning. They seized the time each day to strategize and gossip and dream.

On this particular morning, they ate together as usual in the elegantly appointed private dining room of the company's Century City offices.

A sumptuous repast had been laid out for them. Freddy filled his plate with scrambled eggs, smoked salmon, and a healthy portion of lightly fried plantains. He helped himself to generous servings of tomatoes and mango. He also grabbed several corn tortillas.

Francisco was content to accompany his coffee with a selection of fresh fruit. "How is it you stay so thin yet eat so much?" he asked Freddy.

"Genes."

"How could it be genes? Your parents look like beached whales."

"Then forget genes."

"So?"

"I'm too mean to be fat."

"Too vain is more like it."

The two friends ate in silence for a while.

"Something stinks in Denmark," Freddy said. "You're not gonna like it."

"What am I not gonna like?" Francisco asked as he sipped his coffee.

"Several months ago I was introduced to a Hollywood swell, an apparently well-heeled financial adviser with a habit. An agent for several of his friends, also with habits."

"So?"

"I liked him. He amused me. So I let him in. He made weekly buys. Some weeks better than others. Nothing spectacular."

"Where is this going, Freddy?"

"Guy tried to put the squeeze on me."

"In what way?"

"In a way you won't like."

"Are you going to tell me about it?"

"Only if you promise not to go batshit."

"I promise."

"I don't believe you."

"Let me put it this way. I'm going to count to five and if you haven't told me by the time I finish, I'm going to throw you in the pool."

"I see."

"One," Francisco said.

Freddy didn't say anything.

"Two."

"He's an undercover narc. Claims his assignment is to fuck up the drug deal."

"Why would he tell you that?"

"Because he's bent. He's in business for himself."

"Meaning?"

"He's working both sides of the street."

"What is it he wants?"

"An extra-large payday."

"How extra-large?"

"Very. He also claims not to be working alone. Says there's another agent embedded inside Reyes Enterprises. Says the Feds are planning to bust the meth drop based on information this agent is providing him. Says that for the right price, he'll finger the agent and salvage the meth deal.

"Let me get this straight," Francisco said. "This narc of yours claims there's an undercover agent in our midst who's providing him information regarding the details of our business?"

"Yes."

"How?"

"How what?"

"How does he plan to use that information?"

"He's been instructed to make a significant meth buy. Larger than any he's made before. And when I sanction his buy, he and his LAPD associates will take us down."

"So, don't sell to him."

"That isn't the point."

"What is the point?"

"The guy himself is already irrelevant. He'll be dead by the time the drop is made. What we need from him is the identity of the alleged undercover agent."

"What is it you propose?"

"*Con tu permiso*, I want to extract the name of the agent."

"How?"

"Don't ask."

"What's his protection?"

"Incriminating information on us that he claims will be automatically provided to the Feds should anything happen to him."

"Is it viable?"

"Not to my way of thinking."

"Meaning?"

"Guy's seen too many movies. In real life, all information is

subjective. Existing information becomes invalid when con-
trasting events change things. When informants vanish, for
example. Without informants, all bets are off.

"These riots have muddied things. It's chaos out there. But if
this guy's right, and there's really an implanted agent, we have to
learn who it is and rid ourselves of the threat he poses."

"As always, I leave issues such as these to you, Freddy. You
know this meth deal is too big and too important to go boom."

"I do."

"We can't have anyone undermining our interests."

"I know."

"You're right when you say we need to eliminate this undercover agent."

"It will be done, Frankie. Trust me."

"You're the only person I do trust, Freddy."

"And with good reason."

NINETEEN

After making the rounds in search of him, Freddy found Ryan Scott in the wee hours of Thursday morning, at The Pink Pearl, Hollywood's newest hot spot.

Scott was being entertained by a glamorous hooker in the Oyster Lounge, an exclusive section of the club that offered its special patrons the ultimate privacy of roped-off, curtained booths.

Freddy pulled the curtain aside and stuck his head in.

The hooker was kneeling in front of Scott, performing fellatio on him.

"Hey," Scott bellowed, his eyes half open, his attention focused on the woman. "Get the fuck out of here."

Freddy ignored him. He grabbed the woman's hair and yanked her away from her ministrations. He handed her five hundred dollars and pointed her out of the booth.

As she was leaving, Freddy pressed his finger to his lips and whispered, "Shh."

The woman nodded.

Ryan Scott was livid. "What in the fuck do you think you're doing?"

"You wanted to talk deal?"

"I did, but not now."

"Now's your only chance."

Ryan fumbled with his pants in an effort to make himself presentable.

When Freddy signaled for him to follow, Ryan did.

They stepped out of the club and Freddy pointed to his waiting limousine. "My chariot."

They both climbed into the back seat and sped off into the night.

———

The darkened interior of the limousine made Ryan Scott uncomfortable. He noticed there were two goons in the front seat. He became aware of Freddy's silence. "Where are we going?"

Freddy didn't answer.

"What's happening here?"

Freddy reached inside his jacket pocket and withdrew a switchblade stiletto. He snapped it open and showed it to Ryan, who began to tremble.

"What are you doing?" Ryan murmured.

Freddy swiped the razor-sharp tip of the knife across Ryan's chin.

Ryan gasped and reached for the wound. Blood began to seep through his fingers.

"Just so we understand each other," Freddy said.

Ryan stared at him from frightened eyes.

"Who are you?"

When Ryan didn't respond, Freddy clipped the other side of his chin, which also began to bleed.

"Next time won't be so pretty."

Ryan started to whimper. "I'm with the LAPD narcotics division. Like I told you."

"Name?"

"Ryan Scott."

"Real name?" Freddy asked and showed Scott his stiletto.

"Nicholas Morgan."

"Who's the implanted agent?"

"What about my money?"

"Does it look like I'm going to give you money?"

"If anything happens to me, all of the confidential information I have about you and Reyes Enterprises will fall into police hands."

Freddy shrugged. "Good luck with that," he said.

"I'm serious."

"Wake up, Ryan. Or should I say, Nicholas? Your information's irrelevant. If you have any hope of living longer, I'd advise you to start talking."

Nicholas Morgan backed into the deepest corner of the seat.

Freddy pursued him and stuck his stiletto deep into his arm.

Morgan screamed but said nothing.

Freddy stuck him again, this time in the other arm.

Morgan began to weep.

"I'm only gonna say it once more. Give me the name." Morgan's weeping grew more intense.

Freddy stuck the knife into his side.

Now bleeding profusely and in great pain, Morgan cried out. "Fuck you, Freddy."

Freddy was enraged. Out of control. He slashed Morgan again and again. "I'll finish this now if you don't tell me."

By now, Morgan had lost a great deal of blood. It had pooled on the floor of the limousine. He felt faint.

"Find her yourself," he muttered.

He started to lapse into unconsciousness.

Freddy leaned back in his seat.

"Find her yourself," Freddy mused. "Her."

He hollered to the driver, "Take me home."

He remained silent for the rest of the ride. He paid no heed to the moaning, semiconscious Nicholas Morgan.

When the limousine pulled up in front of his house, Freddy opened his door.

"Wait," Morgan groaned. "What about me?"

"You," Freddy said as if noticing him for the first time. "I'm sorry. I thought you knew. You're already dead."

Then he got out of the limo and slammed the door behind him.

TWENTY

Freddy waited until breakfast to speak with Francisco. He told him all he had learned.

"A woman," Francisco said. "What woman?"

"I have no proof."

"But you have an idea?"

"I do."

"Who?"

"It will hurt you if I speak it."

"It will hurt me more if you don't."

"Kara Machado."

"You're joking."

Freddy sat quietly, allowing Francisco the time to absorb his news.

"Why Kara?" Francisco asked.

"Call it my feminine intuition."

"Which means?"

"She's been with us for what, half a year?"

"Since early October."

"Half a year. And she moved in with you around Thanksgiving."

"She came to Puerto Peñasco with me for Thanksgiving. That's when she met Paco José."

"And that's also when she moved in."

"Yes."

"It wasn't long thereafter that Ryan Scott showed up."

"So?"

"I don't like coincidences," Freddy said.

"So that's why you suspect Kara?"

"Suspect may be too strong a word. Let's just say she's a person of interest. Once Ricardo vets her further, perhaps we'll know more."

"What do you think I should do?"

"To be on the safe side, I've instructed security to immediately seal the enclave and isolate her. Her cell phone and her laptop will be confiscated and carefully examined by our tech team. She will no longer have access to the landlines."

Francisco nodded his assent.

"I've alerted the staff to ready the plane for this evening. So as not to alert the international authorities, I'm having them file a flight plan for Las Vegas. Once you're airborne, the pilots will jam the radar system and communication will be lost. The plane will disappear. You'll be in Puerto Peñasco by morning. We can more closely monitor her there and be worry-free regarding any further leaks."

"And if she's not the one?"

Freddy shrugged.

"I love her, Freddy."

"You will love others, Frankie."

"There won't be any others," Francisco said, turning his face away.

"What would you have me do?"

"Nothing until you are certain."

"I promise nothing more will occur until we know the results of the investigation."

"Should it become necessary," Francisco averred. "I alone will determine the course of action."

"Of course."

"No one else can know."

"No one else will know. But allow me a word of advice?"

"What?"

"You will need to be strong."

TWENTY-ONE

Kara knew something was wrong the moment she opened her eyes. She never fully awakened until after Francisco left for his daily breakfast with Freddy. But today she sensed things were different.

She rang for Maria, her maid, or as Maria liked to be called, her personal assistant.

Maria knocked, and when Kara invited her in, she saw Maria was not alone. She was accompanied by Ricardo Romero, the head of security for Reyes Enterprises.

After making apologies for his unannounced entrance, Romero moved swiftly through the room, seizing Kara's cell phone, her laptop computer, and her iPad.

He bowed obsequiously, then left, closing the door behind him.

Although the swiftness of his actions was startling, Kara knew Romero would find nothing incriminating on any of those devices. She had used none of them to communicate with her handlers.

But she was now forced to acknowledge her position inside the Reyes universe had become tenuous, and possibly even dangerous.

Maria had placed the breakfast tray atop the bedroom table. Now she flung open the curtains and the veranda doors, instantly flooding the spacious room with sunlight and the tart smell of salty sea air.

She never made eye contact with Kara.

"What?" Kara asked.

Maria stopped busying herself. "I'm sorry," she said.

"Sorry for what?"

"It appears you have been placed under house arrest. There are armed guards outside your door. You are no longer allowed to leave the grounds. The phones have been shut off."

"Jesus," Kara said. "What do you know?"

Maria sat on the corner of the bed. She spoke in hushed tones. "Someone has been killed. I don't know who exactly, but rumor has it he was a federal narcotics agent."

"And?"

"There's talk about information leaks. They're hunting for the source of those leaks. That's why there are guards everywhere. I fear this may involve you."

Kara sat silently for a while, deep in thought. She debated whether or not she could rely upon Maria to alert her friends in Los Angeles as to her fate.

She swiftly reached her decision, and whispered to Maria, "I need you to do something for me."

"Please don't get me in any trouble. My family..."

"All I want is for you to remember a phone number."

"Remember it?"

"Yes. I'm going to tell it to you, and I need you to remember it. You cannot write it down. You must commit it to memory."

"All right."

Kara slowly recited the number.

"Why do you want me to remember it?"

"Should anything happen to me... If I am wounded or killed, or I simply disappear, I want you to call the number. But only when it's safe for you to do so. And not from a phone that could be traced."

"And?"

"Ask for a man named Buddy. Tell him everything you know about what may have happened to me. Then hang up."

"And that's all?"

"That's all."

Maria considered Kara's request. She assessed the risk factor both to her and to her family. Uncertain as to whether or not it would actually come to pass, she nonetheless chose to ease Kara's anxiety. "For you I will do this, Kara."

"But only when it's safe for you to do it."

"I understand."

"Thank you, Maria."

"Please look out for yourself, Kara."

"I fully intend to."

TWENTY-TWO

FRIDAY, MAY 1

There was no way I could have known that by the time I finished with Commander Logan and returned home, Kara had already been spirited out of the country.

Following their dinner at Geoffrey's, Francisco and Kara were driven directly to the Santa Monica Municipal Airport where Francisco's Gulfstream IV awaited them.

Despite her protestations, she was hustled aboard by members of the Reyes security team, followed closely by Francisco. The doors were closed, and the plane began to taxi almost immediately. Within minutes, they were airborne.

———

I slept for a while after Betty Jean left.

I awakened at ten thirty, showered, fed Cooper, and brewed some coffee, a cup of which I carried into the living room. I sat down heavily on the sofa. Cooper jumped onto my lap, and I petted him absentmindedly.

I rubbed my stinging eyes and took stock of my situation. My task was to rescue Kara, but I knew little of her circumstances. I was unfamiliar with Paco methodology, but regardless, I didn't believe her life was in any immediate danger. I presumed Reyes would continue to play the role of her protector. At least for the immediate future.

That's not to infer things wouldn't change, but being romantically involved with her, as Francisco clearly was, I couldn't believe him capable of ordering an end to her life.

I gently guided Cooper off my lap, stood, and poured some more coffee. The tinny jangle of my cell phone caught my attention. I answered it. There were several moments of silence.

Then the female voice on the other end of the line said, "Kara asked me to phone you. She has been taken. She was flown out of the country."

"To where? By whom?"

Another silence followed. "I have told you all I know."

Then the line went dead.

TWENTY-THREE

Los Angeles remained a city in crisis.

Commercial air travel was suspended. Train traffic came to a standstill. The curfew remained in effect. All sporting events, concerts, and other forms of entertainment were shut down.

The rioting raged on.

Police from other parts of the state were recruited to assist local authorities. National Guard units took up stations throughout the city. The governor requested federal assistance. The president denounced the rioters.

Since the schools were closed, I arranged for Jimmy to spend the day with Cooper.

Shelley picked me up at noon. We returned to the Mitchum house, where we were joined by Byron Prescott. I told them about the anonymous phone call I had received.

"She gave you no information except to say Kara had been flown out of the country?" Shelley asked.

"Correct."

"She could be anywhere," Byron interjected. "We need to find out how and where she was taken."

"Let me run with that," Shelley said.

"Please do."

She left the den.

I wanted to examine the house more closely, in search of any information it might reveal regarding the activities of Nicholas Morgan. With Byron tagging along, we started with the den. We had just discovered a wall safe when Shelley appeared in the doorway.

"Here's one I'm sure you'll enjoy," she said as she entered and sat down on one of the plush leather sofas. "A Gulfstream IV registered to Reyes Enterprises in Century City was cleared to fly from Santa Monica Airport to McCarran Field in Las Vegas last night. The manifest specified four passengers. Three men and a woman. It took off at 10:24 p.m. and promptly disappeared."

"Disappeared?" Byron exclaimed.

"It vanished from air traffic control radar and hasn't been heard from since."

"Puerto Peñasco," I said. "The pilots must have jammed the radar and flown directly to Sonora."

"No one reported any sightings," Shelley said.

"No one would. Everyone here is on high alert. Distracted. The LA airports are effectively shut down. Planes are being diverted to other locations and flummoxing the system."

"So, what is it you're saying?"

"It's a straight shot to Sonora. I bet there's a private landing field somewhere in the vicinity of Puerto Peñasco and the Paco compound."

"I'll check on it," Shelley said.

She returned to the kitchen.

"Puerto Peñasco," I mused aloud.

"That'd be my guess," Byron said. "Likely she was on the plane. And if so, we're powerless."

"You mean the department is powerless."

"I mean we're powerless. Or to put it more succinctly, you are."

"How so?" I asked.

"We have no authority in Mexico."

"You mean we have no friends there?"

"Friends we have, but we have rules too. We're not authorized to engage in police activities in another country."

"Gee, I must have missed that memo."

"I'm serious, Buddy. There's no way we can cross the border."

"Says you."

"Says the rules. I acknowledge your penchant for independent action, but on this one, you're screwed."

Ignoring Byron's pronouncement, I began nursing a plan of attack.

"I'm going to presume you heard me," Byron said.

"Let's just say I saw your lips moving. I think I need to make a run on Freddy Sunday."

"Meaning?"

"If he wasn't on the plane, I think it's time to rock his boat. Have a few words with him. Loosen his tongue as to what's going on with the Pacos."

Shelley returned to the den. "There's a private landing field in Puerto Peñasco belonging to a company called Crystal M Enterprises."

"They must have had a good laugh when they thought of that name," I chuckled.

"What do you mean?" Byron asked.

"You can't be that dense, Byron."

"Oh, wait. I get it," he said suddenly.

"Too late."

"Shut up, Buddy."

Shelley suppressed a laugh.

Byron glared at her. "So, what are you going to do?" he asked me.

"I'm going to track him down and make the acquaintance of the irrepressible Freddy Sunday."

"Good idea," Byron said. "And you expect to do that how?"

"First I'm going to hit the clubs."

"What clubs? There's a curfew on."

"Not in Malibu," Shelley said. "The clubs there never close."

"You think Freddy is going to show up in Malibu?" Byron asked.

"If that's where the clubs are, that's where he'll be," I told him.

"And of course we'll be there too," Shelley said.

"With the expectation that ol' Freddy and I are going to seize the opportunity to make a little hay together," I said. "I'm going to shiver his timbers. Shiver them until they turn blue."

"You know something, Buddy?" Byron asked.

"What?"

"I haven't a clue as to what in the hell you're talking about."

"Mission accomplished," I snickered.

TWENTY-FOUR

Shelley and I identified ourselves to the management team at Silverado, Malibu's happening nightclub, located in the Cross Creek Country Mart.

After presenting our credentials, we were led to a table in the reserved section.

Silverado was a replica of an old-time Western saloon, replete with a meticulously restored mahogany bar, a sawdust-covered wood plank floor, period furniture, tanned animal hides tacked randomly onto raw wood walls, and a bevy of waitresses, each dressed in skimpy Western garb that called particular attention to the shapely behinds their short skirts barely concealed.

"Are you planning on paying any attention to me at all?" Shelley asked.

"Excuse me?"

"You haven't once been able to stop yourself from ogling that waitress's ass."

"I have no idea what you're talking about."

"Your eyes look like Wile E. Coyote's."

"I'm searching for Freddy Sunday."

"You're trying to determine whether or not she's wearing a thong."

"I am not."

"Of course you are. And she isn't."

"Isn't what?"

"Wearing a thong."

"How do you know?"

"I saw."

"How did you see?"

"She bent over when she set down the bowl of chips."

I considered this for several moments. Then I called out to the waitress. "May we please have another bowl of chips?"

"Unbelievable," Shelley said.

Our attention was suddenly diverted to a minor commotion taking place in front of the club's two swinging doors.

A group of young men and women had entered and were being led to a nearby table that was already set for ten. The boisterous group was seated and immediately began calling for drinks.

A great deal of laughter erupted as the apparent ringleader of the group made some sort of side-of-the-mouth wisecrack.

I knew at once the jokester was Freddy Sunday. He was the center of everyone's attention and basking in it.

He was wearing tight purple toreador pants with a white mariachi shirt tucked into them. The shirt was adorned with large ruffled sleeves.

His prominent cheekbones were heavily rouged. His pale-blue eyes were emphasized by black liner. His pomaded hair was layered in waves and pasted high atop his narrow head. He resembled an outlandishly costumed Lady Gaga.

Freddy's eyes swept the room in search of approbation, as well as a familiar face.

He stopped momentarily to gaze at me.

I blatantly stared back at him.

The light in his eyes momentarily faded, leaving them naked, dead-eyed, venal. Then they quickly regained their luster and moved on.

I leaned over to Shelley and whispered in her ear, "Post time."

She nodded, stood, and exited the club.

After several moments, I meandered over to Freddy's table. When I arrived, I extended my hand. "Freddy, right?" I said.

Freddy's eyes widened. "Do I know you?"

"Buddy."

"I can't quite place you, Buddy."

"I'm crushed."

Freddy grinned. "Remind me."

"I'm Nick Morgan's friend."

Freddy's lighthearted mien immediately faded. "Come again."

"You heard me."

"I'm afraid you'll have to excuse me," Freddy said, turning back to the table.

"Stand up."

"Are you threatening me, sir?" Freddy snarled.

I moved quickly. I grabbed hold of his right hand and before he could react, I cuffed his hands together.

Then I reached for my badge and flashed it at him. "LAPD. On your feet," I instructed.

Freddy started to yell. "What do you think you're doing?"

"Arresting you."

Freddy's table became instantly silent. Everywhere in the room, heads turned to watch.

I hauled Freddy up and out of his chair.

Choke-holding him by the neck, I hustled him out of the restaurant, all the while reciting his rights.

When we stepped outside, he began yelling for his security team. No one responded.

He looked around frantically.

There, lined up beside a Malibu Sheriff's Department cruiser, was his entire security detail. Four soldados, each with his hands bound, each on his knees, facing the cruiser.

"I want my lawyer," Freddy shouted.

I pushed him toward the Mercedes that was parked in front of the club. Shelley was standing beside the open rear door.

I slammed Freddy into the side of the car and patted him down, discovering in the process a small-caliber Seecamp stainless steel pistol, and a switchblade stiletto, both of which I confiscated and placed into evidence bags.

I then moved to shove Freddy into the Mercedes.

When he resisted, I lifted him off his feet and thrust him forcefully inside, smashing his head against the doorframe in the process.

"Oops," I said.

"You'll regret this," Freddy snarled.

"I'll live with it."

I pushed him farther into the vehicle and got in after him.

Shelley closed the door and climbed into the driver's seat.

A crowd had gathered to watch the goings-on. As she fired up the engine, Shelley flashed the onlookers a peace sign.

Then she drove us away.

TWENTY-FIVE

Shelley turned right onto Pacific Coast Highway going north and raced the Mercedes up the winding thoroughfare, slowing only to turn onto Malibu Canyon Road, heading for the hills.

Freddy sat sullenly, staring out the window. Neither Shelley nor I engaged him in conversation.

Several miles ahead, she pulled into the Hilltop Camp parking lot, a summer escape venue for children, as well as the occasional off-season weekend retreat for adults.

The camp was not yet open.

She pulled up to the administration building, facing it squarely, and trained the Mercedes's headlights directly at it.

I pulled Freddy out of the car and stood him in front of the building, where he was illuminated by the car's high-intensity beams.

A night breeze stirred the cool air over the Malibu hills. A half-moon peeked through the heavy cloud cover.

Freddy shivered.

Shelley exited the Mercedes, opened the trunk, and removed a heavy-duty police truncheon. She showed it to Freddy, then leaned back against the front fender of the Mercedes, club in hand, keeping a watchful eye on Freddy.

"Let's get something straight," I said to Freddy. "I know who you are and what you are. I have no interest in how well connected you may be or how many legal advisers you have at your command. I want something from you. And you can be certain I'm going to get it. We can do it the easy way or the hard way. It's up to you."

Freddy glared but said nothing.

I lowered my voice to a near whisper. "I also know how much you cherish your precious appearance. So if you force me to give the order, ol' Shelley over there will smash every bone in your face in order to get what I want. Do we understand each other?"

"What is it you want?" Freddy croaked.

"Information."

"What information?"

"Nicholas Morgan."

"What about him?"

"He was last seen getting into your limousine."

"What of it?"

"Why was he killed?"

"How would I know?"

"Already this isn't going well."

Freddy didn't say anything.

"I'm going to give you one more chance. What was it that caused Nicholas Morgan to be killed?"

The darkened trees moved tremulously in the wind, loosing twigs and leaves that flew haphazardly into the cold night air. A coyote repeatedly wailed a discordant phrase. The chirping of crickets and the occasional frog song completed the cacophony.

Freddy remained silent.

After a few moments, I sighed deeply.

I stepped up to him and, without warning, slapped his face. Back and forth. Hard. Which brought tears to his eyes and a red welt to his cheek.

Then I balled my hand into a fist and reared back as if to punch him in the face.

Freddy screamed, and when he raised his hands in self-defense, I punched him in the stomach.

He fell to the ground, gasping for breath, retching violently. He lay there for several minutes.

Shelley stepped over to Freddy and glared at him with her truncheon in hand. Then she looked at me.

I nodded to her, knelt down, and confronted Freddy.

"Let's try again," I said to him. "Nicholas Morgan."

Clearly frightened, he wheezed out the word, "Bent."

"What bent?"

"Crooked."

Freddy raised himself onto his hands and knees. Then he got to his feet. "You think your American police are less corrupt than the ones we have in Mexico? Keep dreaming, señor. Your friend Mr. Morgan came looking for a payday."

"Which manifested itself how?"

"First tell me what you plan to do with me."

"That depends on you."

"What if I give you the information you seek?"

"It would have to satisfy me."

"And if it does?"

"No harm will befall you."

"How do I know that?"

"You don't."

"And if I say nothing?"

"Shelley will render you unrecognizable."

Freddy thought for a while, then said, "Nicholas Morgan was willing to sell you out."

"Meaning?"

"He was a crook. Once his cover was blown and he proved

to be someone other than the person he had claimed to be, he attempted to extort some serious cash from us. Told us there was a federal agent embedded in our organization. He offered to sell us that agent's name."

"And did he?"

"No."

"Why not?"

"Because he clammed up."

"You refused his offer?"

"We agreed to it. But we didn't have the dough readily available. Without it, he refused to reveal the name."

"So?"

"We held on to him while one of our guys went for the dough."

"And?"

"He must have thought better of it because regardless of the money, he dummied up."

"So you beat it out of him?"

Freddy sneered.

"What exactly did you do to him?" I asked.

"We let him go."

"Sure you did. And pigs fly too."

"Believe what you want."

"You killed him."

"I didn't kill anyone. The Reyeses are not killers."

"Then how did he die?"

"I haven't a clue."

"How did he die, Freddy?"

"He asked to be dropped off in South Central. I guess he hadn't heard about the rioting. I have no idea what happened after he got out of the car."

"You're suggesting he was killed by rioters?"

"I'm suggesting nothing. He was alive and well when he got out of the car."

Fed up with him, I grabbed his nose and twisted it. "Quit lying."

Freddy screamed. "I'm not lying. Nick Morgan told us nothing. He slipped up and called the undercover agent 'she'. But he never gave us her name."

"He never told you her name because she doesn't exist."

Freddy stared at me blank-eyed.

"There is no undercover agent," I said.

"Whatever."

"You killed him."

"I didn't kill him. You think I want the blood of a police officer on my hands? We're a legitimate organization. We don't kill people. I don't kill people. I may be vain, but I'm not stupid."

I looked over at Shelley, who had been standing alongside the car, listening. I nodded to her.

"You're under arrest, Señor Domingo," she said. "A person of interest in the murder of Nicholas Morgan."

"Lucky me."

I frog-marched Freddy back to the car and pushed him inside.

Shelley climbed into the driver's seat, and we made tracks for Parker Center.

TWENTY-SIX

"He loves that dog," Betty Jean said. "We'll be happy to watch him for you."

We were in my apartment. She had been in my bed when I got home. Well after three.

But I was uncharacteristically preoccupied, playing the Freddy Sunday scene over and over in my head.

I was anxious. Restless. Exhausted.

"You're distracted."

I did my best to snap out of it. "I'm sorry."

In an effort to capture my attention, she snuggled up to me. "How long will you be gone?" she asked.

"I'm not sure. Hopefully only a couple of days."

"You'll be in danger?"

My tension had started to drain.

I gently caressed her hair. "I'll be okay."

"What about us?"

"Us?"

"Come on, Buddy. You know what I mean."

"What do you want me to say, Betty Jean?"

"I want to know how you feel about me."

"I'm too young for you."

"I guess that means you think I'm too old for you."

"It means I'm not a good bet for you."

This was far from fresh news. She lay her head on my chest. "I've been thinking of going home," she said.

"Montana?"

"Yes."

"Because?"

"I'm lonely. I'm tired. I have trouble envisioning a future here. Everything feels so transient. And I'm thinking the kids and I would be better off closer to my family."

"Do you want my opinion?"

"You know I do."

"I agree."

"That I would be better off in Montana?"

"Yes."

"And us?"

"I'm not the right guy for you."

"Why do you keep saying that?"

"Because it's true. We love each other. A lot. But not in that way. We're pals, you and I. But we're not life partners. And we both know it."

"I don't know it, Buddy."

"Yes, you do, Betty Jean."

After several moments, she slipped out of her nightie and sensuously climbed on top of me.

She kissed me.

Then she kissed me again.

I put my arms around her.

She lowered herself and sought me.

She shifted position and found me.

She shuddered.

"I sure do like this, though," she whispered.

"What's not to like?"

TWENTY-SEVEN

SATURDAY, MAY 2

We were seated in Commander Logan's office. It was eight a.m.

Four thousand soldiers were pouring into the city. The mayor came on television to assure the populace the riots were effectively over and the heightened military presence would ensure the return of tranquility and order.

The Justice Department announced it was launching an investigation of the entire affair.

A peace march had been hastily organized for later that afternoon. The worst was clearly over.

Shelley, Murray Goodman, Byron Prescott, and I were present. Logan, weary and spent, sat listening as I explained the events of last evening.

"I've already had five calls from three different attorneys at Steinberg, Steinberg, and Greenberg," Goodman said.

"Sounds like a Groucho Marx law firm," I said.

"We're all pretty tired around here, Buddy," Goodman said. "Is there any chance you could can the comedy?"

"Should we believe Freddy Sunday?" Byron asked.

"Freddy Sunday or his minions killed Nicholas Morgan. No question," I stated. "Likely under torture, Morgan may have spilled the beans regarding Kara. But he didn't reveal her identity. She may be under suspicion, but there's no certainty. Sunday is painting a picture of Morgan as a bad cop who placed a fellow officer in a life-threatening situation. He's lying."

"Is that what you want me to tell the Steinberg firm?" Goodman asked.

"Tell the Steinberg firm their client is a cold-blooded killer. Point them to the district attorney's office."

"How do we explain a rogue cop who kidnapped their client and threatened him with disfigurement?"

"You mean me?"

"If the shoe fits," Goodman said.

I turned to Commander Logan. "Is he always like this?"

"What now, Buddy?" Logan asked.

"I say we look at things from Kara Machado's perspective."

"Which is?"

"She's being held against her will by Francisco Reyes. She was herded onto a plane and flown out of the country, a clear violation of her civil rights. In all likelihood she's currently under some sort of house arrest in Mexico. She doesn't know whether or not she's ticketed for execution. She has every reason to be terrified."

"You think?" Goodman said.

I stared at Murray Goodman and shook my head. Then I turned to Logan. "Does our agreement still stand?"

Logan nodded.

"Then I'd like to discuss our next course of action."

"I'm listening."

"So is Murray. I'd like to invite him out."

"He is my deputy."

"Then surely there are other issues that require his attention."

"With all due respect, sir," Goodman said. "I think…"

"It's not working," Logan interrupted. "The two of you are like oil and water."

Goodman stood. He looked around the room, gathered his papers, and headed for the door.

Then he turned to me. "I hope for Kara's sake you don't fuck this up."

"Thanks for your support."

Goodman looked at me for a few seconds more, then left the room.

"All right," Logan said. "what's your plan?"

TWENTY-EIGHT

We were sprawled out on various pieces of furniture in the den, which we had come to regard as our clubhouse. Shelley was drinking a Coke. Byron had a root beer. I was sipping coffee. It was just after ten a.m.

The encroaching heat of the day was tempered by the cool of the den. Streams of sunlight poured through the dormer windows but were deflected by the wooden slats of the Venetian blinds.

Dust motes danced in the light shafts. The harsh sound of crows cawing disrupted the quiet.

An aura of lassitude had settled upon us. Shelley was yawning. My eyes were half closed. Only Byron remained alert and on guard. "So when will you be leaving?" he asked.

"Shortly," I said.

"And you're still unwilling to reveal your destination?"

"Correct."

"And you're not telling us because…"

"Because it's personal."

"Personal? Here we are in the midst of a crisis procedure, and you're about to disappear for several hours on personal business."

"Correct."

"This afternoon," Byron said.

"This afternoon what?"

"What time this afternoon?"

"I'm scheduled to arrive in Yuma in time for the four o'clock meeting."

"Can you at least tell us where you'll be arriving from?"

"No."

"This was no easy thing to arrange."

"I appreciate that."

"The governor will be plenty pissed if you don't show."

"Ye of little faith."

"Stop saying that. I've staked a large portion of my reputation on this."

"If we're successful, your reputation will be greatly enhanced."

"It's not enhancement I'm worried about. If this thing goes south, everyone will blame me."

"Why don't you look at it from a different perspective?"

"What perspective?"

"You're a police officer. You've been recruited to participate in a high-risk operation. For the first time in your career, you'll be able to move your fat ass out from behind a desk and actually participate in an important operation."

"It's not fat."

"What?"

"My ass. It's not fat."

"You know what I mean."

Shelley sat up and looked around, as though she had just awakened, which, in reality, she had. "Tell me you're not still bickering."

"Buddy won't let on as to where he's going," Byron said.

"So what? Do we really care?"

"I do."

"Give it a rest, Byron," she said.

"Hey. It wasn't you who convinced the governor of Sonora to ignore protocol and surreptitiously escort us across the border."

Shelley yawned. "I'm sure he's got his reasons."

"I still don't like it."

I rearranged myself on the sofa and took a large gulp of coffee. "We meet at four. Does the governor know we want to be in Puerto Peñasco before sunset?"

"He does," Byron said.

"Tell us about the hacienda again."

"It's situated on Calle Pancho Villa, within sight of the Reyes compound."

"Remind me."

"It fronts a private beach."

"And?"

"It has its own dock."

"Where a boat can be moored."

"Yes."

"Walled and guarded?"

"As promised. It belongs to a political ally of the governor's. When he's not in residence, it's sometimes used to entertain visiting dignitaries. It's not unusual for strangers to come and go."

"Watched by the Pacos?"

"Everything in Puerto Peñasco is watched by the Pacos."

More so since the arrest of Freddy Sunday, I mused.

His legal team had argued successfully for his release. No proof. No priors. No jail time. I feared for Kara's safety. Despite any impending danger, I was eager to be on the scene. Confident of my plan. Anxious to put it into effect.

"We'll cross the border at Yuma," Byron said. "The drive shouldn't take more than a couple of hours, and if we time it properly, we'll arrive at dusk as planned."

"Our cover?"

"You and Shelley are rumored to be relatives of one of the governor's big contributors. Which earned you a two-day hacienda holiday as his guests."

"And the staff?"

"They've been briefed you'll be in residence for only a short time. You are to be afforded every privilege. I'll serve as the liaison, assigned to ensure your comfort and privacy."

"That's good work, Byron."

"What time do you need to be at the airport?" Shelley asked when she saw me gaze at my watch.

"No airport."

"What?"

"I'm driving."

"You're driving?"

"Actually I'm being driven."

"Driven by whom?"

"By the party who should be buzzing the gate momentarily."

"I hate all this intrigue," Byron said.

"It's for the best," I said.

"I still don't like it."

The intercom rang. I stood, stretched, then went to the box and pressed the intercom button. "Buddy," I said.

"It's me," came the reply.

I punched in the gate code.

I signaled for the others to remain where they were. "I'll see you at four."

Then I picked up my bag and left the house.

TWENTY-NINE

The elevator doors opened, and Mary Steel stepped out.

At first she didn't see me, which allowed me a moment to regard her.

She wasn't her vibrant self any longer. The dementia had taken its toll. Now that she was in the assisted-living facility, the last vestiges of her youth had vanished.

Her once-buoyant brown hair was gray and drab. She was wearing a frayed yellow housedress and a gnarled waistpack. She walked slowly, without purpose. She lacked energy. She projected an aura of weariness.

Her vacant eyes brightened when she spotted me. We hugged each other, and she leaned back to look at me.

"You're too thin," she said.

"Ditto," I said.

We walked arm in arm through the lobby of the facility and stepped outside into the warm spring air.

Betty Jean saw us emerge and got out of her Chevy Malibu. She opened the back door and Cooper leapt from the car. He made a beeline for Mary.

She knelt down to hug him. He slobbered wet kisses all over her.

I looked at Betty Jean, who smiled.

Mary stood, and, with Cooper at her side, she stepped over to Betty Jean and embraced her.

"Hello, Mary," Betty Jean said. "You look wonderful."

"Please. I'm a sorry sight and I know it."

"Not true," I said. "You look great, Mom."

We walked from the parking lot to a garden that offered shade and comfortable benches.

Mary sat, and Cooper immediately leapt onto the bench, settled down beside her, and rested his head on her lap.

Betty Jean and I sat opposite them.

A warm breeze stirred the branches of the eucalyptus and palm trees. A pair of gray doves chased each other playfully through them. A siren could be heard in the distance.

"I miss him," she said pointing to Cooper. "He's my special pal."

She petted him and scratched his big ears. She held his face in her hands so as to look into his eyes. She hugged him.

"I wish I was still in the house."

"It wasn't possible any longer, Mom. It was too hard for you to manage."

"I had those meals-on-wheels."

"Which you often forgot to eat."

"I wasn't always hungry."

"Please let's not go over this again. We agreed living here was the best thing for you."

"I wish Cooper could live with me."

"You know he can't."

"Look at him," she said pointing to the big bloodhound. "He wants to be with me as much as I want to be with him. Why can't you make it happen, Buddy?"

"I'm doing the best I can, Mom."

"Don't be short with me, Buddy. You'll be rid of me soon enough."

"No one wants to be rid of you, Mom. This is a very fine facility. They take very good care of you."

We sat silently for a while, watching as Mary tenderly hugged and petted Cooper.

"I made detective grade," I said.

"Like father, like son," she murmured.

Then she brightened. "Did you bring it?"

"It's right here," I said and handed her the plastic bag I had carried to the bench with me.

She peeked inside. "Macallan's twelve-year single malt," she gloated. "My favorite."

"Don't let them see it."

"They won't," she averred as she stuffed the bottle of whiskey deep into her waistpack.

I glanced at my watch. "We have to go, Mom."

"But you just got here."

"I need to be on time for my shift."

"You should have come earlier."

"I'm sorry."

We walked back to the main building. Mary knelt and gave Cooper a final hug.

Then she hugged Betty Jean. She looked at me.

I took her in my arms.

"I have so much trouble remembering things," she whispered.

"You're doing great, Mom. I couldn't be more proud of you."

"Do you really mean that, Buddy?"

"You know I do."

She managed a weak smile. "Will I see you next week?"

"I wouldn't miss it for anything."

"I wish Cooper could be with me."

"I know," I said and kissed her. "They're taking very good care of you."

"You're such a fine son, Buddy."

"I love you, too, Mom."

———

I loaded Cooper into the Malibu and climbed in after him.

Once we were secure, Betty Jean headed out. "LAX?" she inquired.

"Burbank."

"What do you think?"

"About Mom?"

Betty Jean nodded.

"I wish she was better."

"She's so comforted by Cooper. Is there any news?"

"About the venue change?"

"Yes."

"I'm working on it."

"And?"

"The medical team there has signed off on it."

"Meaning?"

"She meets their criteria. She's acceptable to them."

"And Cooper?"

"Him too."

"And she doesn't know?"

"Hasn't a clue."

"Why not?"

"Because I'd hate to disappoint her."

"You mean if it fell through?"

"Exactly."

"So it will come to her as a surprise?"

"A big surprise."

"When?"

"Soon."

"Is there anything I can do?"

"Yeah. Keep your fingers crossed."

THIRTY

Kara sensed Francisco's hesitancy. Whereas he had always been forthright and assertive, he was now tentative, laid-back, very un-Francisco-like.

Following their arrival at the compound in Puerto Peñasco, Francisco hadn't accompanied her to bed. It was only after he thought she was asleep that he quietly entered their spacious quarters and slipped under the sheets. He made no move toward her.

She guessed she was under suspicion, surmising someone had alerted Team Paco to the likelihood of a mole in their operation. But she felt certain she had yet to be identified as that mole.

Her training had prepared her for the possibility of discovery. She had been taught the finer points of defense and escape. She was highly skilled in the martial arts, and on the basis of her belt grade, was considered a lethal weapon.

What she hadn't counted on was becoming a prisoner in a foreign country. Her support systems were unavailable to her. She was isolated and held incommunicado. She needed to find a way to deflect suspicion away from herself.

Although she had given a clear signal to Buddy when he made his surprise appearance at Geoffrey's, she had no hope he would come to her aid in Mexico.

It was left solely to her to find a way out or, in all likelihood, die trying.

Francisco stirred and his eyes flickered opened. They focused on her, sitting beside him.

She smiled at him. "You came to bed late."

"Unfinished business."

"I always forget how beautiful it is here. Will you have time to swim?"

"Perhaps after my meetings."

She yawned and stretched her arms above her head.

Then she slipped out of her negligee revealing her slender, sensuous body.

Francisco watched her.

She moved to his side. She pulled the covers off him, revealing his own nakedness. She stared at him. Then she climbed on top of him and positioned herself so that the tips of her breasts brushed his chest.

She shifted restlessly, insinuating her pert nipples into his moist lips.

He stirred beneath her.

She reached for him and encountered his hardness. He thrust himself against her.

She guided him inside.

His uncertainty vanished. He became forceful and insistent.

He turned her onto her back and reestablished their rhythm.

He paid close attention to her needs, and when they were fulfilled, he satisfied his own.

Afterward they lay quietly, holding each other as if they were one.

"You had me worried," she said.

"How so?"

"I can't remember a time when we didn't come to bed together."

"I was distracted."

"So I noticed. But you weren't distracted this morning."

He laughed. "No, I most assuredly wasn't."

THIRTY-ONE

After he left, Kara got out of bed and opened the shutters. She stepped onto the veranda which afforded a panoramic view of the white sand beach and beyond it, the sun-speckled waters of the Gulf of California.

The morning was pleasantly mellow. The already-cloudless sky promised a sultry afternoon.

Puerto Peñasco was becoming more of a tourist destination. New shops and restaurants had sprung up on the boulevards. A Marriott resort hotel was readying itself for a summer opening. A plethora of construction sites now adorned the once-deserted beachfront and overwhelmed the quiet with the sounds of vehicular traffic, heavy machinery, vehicles, and raised voices.

She looked around at the Reyes family compound. It had been built long ago, at a time when there were no other houses on the beach.

Legend had it the Reyes brothers, Paco José and Paco Luis, had come upon it when they first arrived in Puerto Peñasco and instantly determined it had to be theirs.

They approached the owner and offered a price that was

deemed unacceptable. They increased the offer. The owner declined once again and then refused to discuss it further.

It was long rumored that the owner disrespected the two Pacos by slamming the door in their faces.

Whether or not that was in fact the case, the offending owner was found a few days later, his battered body having washed ashore, the cause of death undetermined.

When another member of the offending family also died suddenly, the survivors quickly relented, and the two brothers purchased the property for considerably less than the sum they had originally offered.

The beachfront compound now consisted of two separate mansions, both built by the Pacos, both constructed to withstand the relentless struggle with the unpredictable effects of the sea.

Over time, as their fortunes increased, the Reyes brothers made considerable improvements to the sizable property. They landscaped it beautifully with native plants and indigenous trees. Flower gardens were planted everywhere.

They constructed a pair of swimming pools, the smaller of the two for the children, the Olympic-sized pool for the exclusive use of the grown-ups.

They laid in a Pancho Segura–designed tennis court. Servants quarters were added. And most importantly, they constructed a massive concrete wall that entirely surrounded it all, providing impenetrability and a comforting sense of security.

Kara slipped into a bathing suit, grabbed a beach towel, and headed downstairs for a swim.

When she arrived at the French doors that led to the beach, she encountered a pair of armed guards who insisted upon accompanying her.

She paid them little mind and wended her way along the

garden pathway toward the wooden boardwalk that trailed through the wind-whipped sand dunes.

She made her way to the beach, the guards following.

When she reached the shore, she dropped her towel and dove into the surf.

The guards stood in her wake, watching from the shore as she plunged into the bay.

The cool water was refreshing, and she swam with strength and agility. After a while she flipped onto her back and began to float, her face turned to the sun, her body buoyed by the salty sea.

She became aware of the guards calling out her name, beckoning her to return. She ignored them. She headed north, swimming parallel to the shore.

The guards ran after her, struggling with the weight of their clothing and their heavy shoes, which kept sinking into the soft, hot sand, throwing them off-balance.

Kara soon realized she had left the guards behind.

They stood helplessly by, watching as she slipped farther and farther away.

She had a momentary thought of flight, but brushed it aside, aware that the Pacos were the power in Puerto Peñasco, and there was little likelihood she could successfully engineer an unplanned escape.

She headed back down the coast toward the compound.

When she reached Fortress Paco, she was surprised to discover not only the two guards who had been chasing her, but a cadre of several others, all of them lining the shore.

She climbed out of the water, picked up her towel, and began to dry herself.

One of the guards approached her and grabbed her roughly by the arm. He was mean-looking and wiry, reeking of unpleasantness and impatience. His hooded eyes were like dark, angry coals peering out at her from a weathered face that had been permanently scarred by deeply etched acne pits.

He yelled at her. "What do you think you were doing?"

His fingers were like a vise on Kara's arm. She wrenched herself from his grasp.

Furious, she stepped up to him and without warning, karate chopped his neck and then kneed him hard in the balls.

The guard's face first registered surprise, then outrage, then pain as he fell to his knees onto the hot sand.

"How dare you put you put your hands on me," she snarled. She spat into his upturned face.

He glared at her but didn't speak.

She spun away from him, kicking sand in his face as she did so.

She walked quickly to the house, passing the assembled guards without so much as a glance.

When she entered the compound she encountered Francisco's father, Paco José Reyes, who had been watching the events on the beach.

A broad grin appeared on his pale face. "Kara, Kara," the old man said. "Remind me to never anger you."

"Don Paco," she said.

She hugged the old patriarch, who hugged her back and while so doing, ran his hand slyly along the curve of her behind.

"Ach," she said, stepping away from him and making as if to slap his hand. "You're incorrigible. Aren't you too old for such nonsense?"

"I may be old, but I'm not dead."

Although Kara laughed at his joke, she found the don's appearance alarming. Once regal in posture and mien, he now bore the freight of his illness.

He had lost a great deal of weight. The skin on his colorless

face hung flaccidly. He moved slowly. He appeared exceptionally frail.

He guided her to the veranda, where a table had been freshly
laid for them.

As they sat, a bevy of servants rushed forward, carrying cups
of freshly brewed coffee and a basket of sweet rolls fresh from
the oven.

"Who is that horrible man?" Kara asked.

"I think I've seen him before," Don Paco said. "It appears as if
he underestimated you."

"He's lucky I didn't do worse."

"I'll see to it he's removed from our service. Just as soon as
the feeling returns to his nuts."

She laughed.

They sipped their coffee.

Kara tore off a sliver of sweet roll and swiftly devoured it.
"How is it?" she asked.

The old man sighed. "The cancer is the cancer. I am still with
the chemo, and most of the time I feel poorly."

"I'm sorry."

Don Paco gazed at the sea, his thoughts seemingly eons away.
"I haven't much time."

"You can't really know that, Paco. The chemo could all of a
sudden turn things around."

"I know how I feel, Kara," the old man said, then added, "Be
good to him. He loves you."

He took hold of her hand and held it tightly for a while. Then
he pushed his chair away from the table and, with some difficulty, managed to stand. "It is time for rest."

He leaned down and kissed the top of her head. "You cheer
me, Kara."

She smiled at him.

He slowly made his way into the house.

Kara finished her coffee and then she, too, headed inside.

One of the guards bowed to her as she passed. She took no notice.

She went upstairs to her quarters and locked the door behind her. She removed her bathing suit and took a long hot shower. Afterward, she dried herself, wrapped a towel around her head, and slipped into a terrycloth bathrobe.

She picked up a book and stepped onto the veranda.

She stared at the sea and was immediately caught up in the plight of an agitated gull who kept diving for fish but always emerged with an empty beak.

Then she noticed the soldado—the one she had kicked.

He was standing alone in the sand dunes, staring up at her.

She shuddered and took a step backward. For the first time she experienced a pang of fear.

Then she turned away and walked to the sheltered sunporch. Once there, she removed her robe and applied ample amounts of lotion to her pale, naked body.

Settling herself into an overstuffed chaise and absorbing the warmth of the midday sun, she closed her eyes and considered her options for escape.

THIRTY-TWO

Having been assured by his legal team he was cleared to travel, Freddy Sunday arrived in Puerto Peñasco in the late afternoon.

Members of his family were at the airport to greet him and welcome him home.

His mother was preparing a dinner of his favorite foods. His three adoring sisters fawned over him, excitedly speculating on his appearance at dinner, arguing about which of his singularly eccentric outfits he might wear.

His father embraced his only son and wondered anew how he could have sired such a creature.

The Domingo family was once again whole.

Before dinner, Freddy walked the short distance from his family's villa to the Reyes compound and once there, he and Francisco ventured into the solarium, where they were served cold drinks and hot empanadas.

"The riots are officially over," Freddy said, between sips of icy sangria.

"And the drop?" Francisco asked.

"If you approve, we're considering it for late next week."

"It will be safe?"

"Once the military presence eases, it will be safe."

"Which should be when?"

"They're saying Monday."

"We'll decide then."

The two men sat quietly, accustoming themselves anew to the relaxing influence of the sultry heat and humidity. The air smelled of salt spray and seaweed, with a tinge of the aroma of newly mowed grass. This was the environment of their childhoods, and they relished it.

"It's good to be home," Freddy said.

"How was your journey?"

"Not without its mishaps."

"Oh?"

"Soon after you left, I was arrested."

"Arrested?"

"By some young punk of a cop who was seeking information regarding the death of Ryan Scott. Or should I say Nicholas Morgan, which was his real name."

"How was he able to do this?"

"He detained my security team, then he stuffed me in his car and drove me into the hills above Malibu."

"And?"

"He wanted to learn what we know."

"About the undercover agent?"

"Yes."

"And?"

"I told him Morgan had attempted to squeeze us. That he was crooked."

"And?"

"He listened."

"What did you tell him we knew?"

"That Morgan maintained it was a woman who had been

implanted. The cop said Morgan was full of shit. He denied any such agent had been insinuated into our operations. He insisted it was I who killed Nicholas Morgan, and he arrested me."

"I'm sorry."

"It was what it was. The Steinberg firm stepped in and had me immediately released."

"What more do we know?"

"About the alleged mole?"

"Yes."

"Still nothing certain. Ricardo and his team have narrowed the investigation to three possible suspects. I'm hopeful they'll know something definitive by tomorrow."

Francisco didn't say anything for a while. Then he asked, "You're still making Kara for this?"

"I'm reserving judgment until I hear from Ricardo. Why? What are you thinking?"

"I don't know, Freddy. It's complicated. It's hard for me to believe it could be her. Plus, she's a great favorite of my father's, and he's heartened by her presence. He's not doing well, and she comforts him."

Francisco distractedly picked up a shrimp from the plate of hors d'oeuvres and gave it the once-over. Then he put it back down.

"She's no dope," he said. "She's aware something is amiss. She had an incident with a member of the security team."

"Oh?"

"She embarrassed him in front of the men. My father wants him dismissed."

"Which one was it?"

"Esteban Marco."

"You're going to fire him?" Freddy asked.

"I don't have much choice. If I don't honor my father's wishes, he'll become curious as to why not."

"I hope this ends well, Francisco. For your sake."

"I know."

"I wish I wasn't so uneasy about it."

"I know."

The two men stood. They embraced. "You'll be here for dinner?"

"For dessert."

"Wear something sane," Francisco said.

"I was thinking of a *Blue Lagoon* sarong and the Madonna headdress."

"Perfect."

"You think?"

Francisco punched him lightly in the arm. "No."

"Peasant," Freddy chided.

THIRTY-THREE

I arrived in Yuma in time for our appointment.

The three of us settled into the private dining room at Pancho Villa's, a trendy southwestern-style cantina, located in Old Town.

In addition to the best green corn tamales in all of Arizona, Villa's boasted of its generously poured mojitos, which we were currently enjoying.

"No more than one," Byron said.

"I don't know about you, but these are too good to stop at just one," I said.

"Please don't embarrass me in front of the governor."

"Define embarrass."

"I knew this was a mistake."

Shelley suddenly signaled to the waiter. *"Uno mas. Con chips."*

"That does it," Byron said. "I'm calling the whole thing off."

"Relax. Just because you can't handle more than one doesn't mean that Shelley and I can't."

"Oh, please. You'll be face-first in the guacamole before he even gets here."

There was a commotion at the door to the private dining

room. We looked up in time to see a large man in a white suit step inside. The man spotted Byron and waved. Then he headed for the table, all smiles and handshakes.

Governor Ignacio Ubaldo Beltran y Chavez was indeed a big man, heavy of body, sporting an oversize head that seemed too large even for his frame.

He carried the Resistol straw cowboy hat he had removed when he entered the dining room. He wore a pair of spit-shined snakeskin boots. A large, droopy mustache was the centerpiece of his crooked face. His eyes sparkled with a lively intelligence.

"Don Byron," the governor said, "it is so very nice to see you once again."

Byron stood and introduced Governor Chavez to Shelley and me.

"Thank you for coming so far north to meet us," I said. "We are most appreciative."

The governor smiled, expectantly.

Byron reached into his jacket and surreptitiously produced a small manila envelope and handed it to Governor Chavez, who nodded his thanks.

"In Mexico, we have a great many palms that require the grease," the governor said.

"In America too," Byron said.

"Not so many, I think."

"You'd be surprised."

A waiter came and took the governor's drink order. I joined Shelley in a second mojito.

Byron stared daggers at us.

"Tell me again how I may be of service," the governor asked Byron, who in turn, outlined the plan.

Before he finished, the waiter took our sumptuous dinner

order and provided Governor Chavez with a second mojito and, subsequently, a third.

I grinned at Byron.

The dinner progressed as planned, and once it ended, we three Americans accompanied the governor to his waiting limousine and piled into it with him.

The governor's entourage included a number of official-looking vehicles that, along with the limousine, resembled a small motorcade as it sped off toward the border.

Although the accompanying vehicles were stopped for inspection, the governor's limousine was waved through customs with barely a glance.

When we reached the border town of San Luis Rio Colorado, the motorcade pulled to a stop in front of the newly constructed city hall.

The three of us climbed out.

We gathered our luggage and waved our thanks to Governor Chavez, whose limo then sped away.

We got into the Ford Explorer a member of the governor's staff had arranged for us and drove off, heading south on the road to Puerto Peñasco.

THIRTY-FOUR

In Los Angeles, Murray Goodman reported his most recent findings to Commander Jeremy Logan.

The LAPD Nerd Squad, as it had come to be known within the department, had finally hacked its way into the Reyes Enterprises mainframe and successfully invaded its employee files.

There the hackers found two candidates who matched the profile they had been seeking. Both were women, of course. Both had joined the company within a handful of months on either side of the time Kara Machado had begun to work there.

Once inside, the hackers chose Wanda Rodriguez as their targeted employee and set about reinventing her biography, leaving behind a questionable past that was bound to catch the attention of anyone who might inspect her file.

New information was inserted into Rodriguez's résumé, buried in her legitimate employment history.

In the newly configured bio, Rodriguez's job history now included a period of employment at the Drug Enforcement Agency, an entity which, at the very least, would raise a few eyebrows and temporarily deflect attention away from Kara.

At Logan's behest, Goodman had been authorized to have Rodriguez picked up and held incommunicado at the female detention center in Santa Monica. No charges were brought against her.

It was Logan's intention to hold her until the Puerto Peñasco operation was resolved. Then he would arrange to have her released, informing her that she had been mistakenly held.

This information reached Byron Prescott just prior to his arrival in Yuma.

———

Freddy Sunday got the news late in the day on Saturday.

Ricardo Romero, the head of security for Reyes Enterprises, had uncovered a puzzling piece of information in the employment history of one Wanda Rodriguez, an administrative assistant, information that linked her to the Drug Enforcement Agency.

Ricardo was curious as to why this information hadn't been vetted when Rodriguez was originally hired, but it was his intention to delve more deeply into it now.

Ricardo told Freddy there would be somewhat of a delay in his investigation because Wanda Rodriguez herself was nowhere to be found. He was assuming she had left town when the riots broke out and would return in time for work on Monday. But until she surfaced, his investigation would be stalled.

Freddy thanked him and reported the news to Francisco.

"So it's possible Kara isn't the one?" Francisco queried.

"It's possible."

"Who exactly is Wanda Rodriguez?"

"One of the assistants."

"Do I know her?"

"I don't even know her. Which has to be a sign she's not ter-ribly attractive."

"Are you suggesting I only notice the good-looking assistants?"

"I'm not only suggesting, I'm attesting."

"Sexist."

"Everything I am I learned from you."

THIRTY-FIVE

Shelley and I parked within sight of the main gates of the thickly walled Reyes compound.

I lowered the Explorer's windows, allowing the sea breezes and the damp night air to surround us and infect our senses.

It was Saturday evening, and we had begun our surveillance soon after arriving in Puerto Peñasco.

Byron had remained at the hacienda, making certain the arrangements there met with his satisfaction.

The evening had thus far been uneventful. Apart from the appearance of a lone delivery boy riding a bike, no one had either entered or exited the compound.

We kept up our chatter, as much to stay awake as to actually communicate. It had been a long week, one marked by limited amounts of sleep.

"You happy with all this?" she asked.

"With all what?"

"With me."

"You mean am I happy with you as a partner?"

"Yes."

"I am."

"Really?"

"Insecure, are we?"

"You don't exactly exude a whole lot of signals."

"What kind of signals would you want?"

"Signals as to whether or not you're happy with me."

"I just gave you a signal."

"Which I had to yank out of you."

"So you think I'm uncommunicative?"

"I didn't say that."

"But do you?" I asked again.

She shrugged.

"Do you?"

"If the shoe fits…"

"I think you're a good partner."

"People haven't always felt that way."

"I can't imagine why."

"Nor can I."

"Maybe it's a guy thing," I said. "Guys sometimes feel uncomfortable around women. Especially if they're intelligent and qualified women."

"Guys like Steve Marshall," she said.

"Your ex?"

"I think he was threatened by me."

"I think he was threatened by himself."

"Why would you say that?"

"I knew Steve Marshall. Admittedly he was a nice guy and an okay cop. Well-meaning and all."

"But?"

"You said something about a secret."

"I did."

"He definitely had a secret," I said.

"Yes, he did."

"Which you probably exacerbated."

"More than probably."

"Are you over him?"

"Pretty much."

"You still think about him?"

"Some."

"You ever hear from him?"

"He moved to San Francisco. Big gay community. He made a life for himself. He fit in. I'm happy for him, but he sure left me a constant reminder of himself."

"Hartman the Heartless?"

"Someone comes up with it every day. And when they don't actually say it, they think it."

We sat silently for a while.

"Look," Shelley said suddenly.

She pointed to the roadway in front of the villa.

"There," she said.

Approaching the main gates were Francisco Reyes and Freddy Sunday. They were unaccompanied by any security personnel. But they were accompanied by Kara Machado.

Freddy and Francisco were engaged in animated conversation. Kara walked silently behind them, scuffing up the dust with her sneakers.

The two villa gates swung open and the three of them disappeared inside. The gates closed behind them.

"Bingo," I said.

"At least we know she's alive."

"What a relief."

After several moments, Shelley said, "I brought you something."

"What?"

"A gift."

"You brought me a gift?"

"Of sorts."

"Do you want to present it to me?"

"I'm thinking about it."

"You're thinking about presenting me with the gift you brought for me?"

"Yes."

"But you're uncertain as to whether or not you'll actually give it to me."

"Yes."

"And that seems sane to you?"

"Don't badger me, Buddy."

"Badger you?"

"Yes."

"Why is this so difficult?" I said, looking skyward.

"It's not exactly an item I should be presenting to you."

"Why not?"

"Because it's confiscated property."

"Confiscated from whom?"

"Freddy Sunday."

"You have a gift for me which was confiscated from Freddy Sunday?"

"Yes."

"What is it?"

"His stiletto switchblade."

"His knife?"

"Yes. It tested negative. It had already been thoroughly cleaned."

"How did you get it?"

"Forensics returned it to me."

"Why didn't you keep it in evidence?"

"I thought you might like it."

"Why would you think that?"

"Because you were the one who confiscated it."

"As evidence."

"Yes. But it's not really evidence. By rights it should be returned to its owner."

"But you're giving it to me instead."

She smiled and handed me the switchblade.

I studied it for a while. It had been forged out of heavy-duty blue steel. Its spring mechanism and its balance had been expertly engineered. It was beautiful to behold, but it was also a frightening implement of disfigurement and death.

"Scary," I said. "Lethal."

We both noticed the villa gates swing open.

We saw Freddy Sunday pass through them, accompanied by another man, a wiry individual, ominous-looking even from afar.

The two men strode away from the compound. Their conversation appeared to be contentious. The wiry man was waving his arms in the air, pointing and gesticulating in apparent agitation.

He stepped in front of Freddy and bumped him with his chest.

Freddy pushed him away.

Then Freddy reached into his pocket and withdrew what appeared to be the twin of the stiletto switchblade Shelley had just given to me. He obviously had more than one.

Freddy released the spring mechanism, and the blade snapped open. He showed it to the wiry man, who raised his arms as if in surrender and then stepped back.

After glaring at him for several moments, Freddy turned and walked swiftly in the opposite direction.

The man watched him go.

Then he began to walk slowly in the direction of the Explorer in which Shelley and I were sitting.

Deep in thought, he passed the darkened Explorer without noticing us inside. He disappeared around a corner.

"What do you think that was about?" Shelley asked.

"Beats me."

"Looked like he had some kind of beef with Freddy."

"It did, didn't it?"

Again we sat silently.

It was late.

We had been prepared to knock off at around midnight, which had already come and gone.

I yawned and stretched. "Have we done it?"

"Are you thinking about sleep as much as I am?"

"More."

I was just about to fire up the engine when the wiry man reappeared and walked hurriedly around the corner, heading back toward the villa.

Once there, he knocked on the gates.

They opened.

A security officer stepped out. After a brief conversation, the guard stepped aside, and the wiry man entered the compound. The guard followed, and the gates closed behind him.

Shelley looked at me questioningly.

"I haven't a clue," I said.

Then I shrugged, revved up the Explorer, and headed for the hacienda.

———

Esteban Marco secreted himself in a little-used storage closet, adjacent to Francisco's quarters.

He was livid. First the little bitch humiliated him in front of his men. Then Freddy dressed him down and fired him.

Marco had been personally recruited for his position and championed by Paco Luis Reyes, who was now living in retirement in Australia.

With the old man gone, Esteban had no one to whom he could appeal. When he pleaded with Freddy to keep his job, the bastard pulled a knife and threatened him with it.

All Marco could think about was revenge.

He had hurried to his parked car in order to collect the Glock semiautomatic pistol he kept hidden in it.

Then he returned to the compound and convinced Mauricio Gonzales, his friend and fellow security officer, to allow him access, presumably to collect his belongings.

But once inside, Esteban headed for the storage closet.

He waited there for daybreak and the moment when Francisco Reyes would leave the bedroom and go downstairs for breakfast.

Francisco's puta would then be alone in the room.

Marco's mind was filled with thoughts of how he would exact his revenge upon her.

Finally, at dawn, Francisco gently closed the door behind him and headed for the kitchen.

Esteban Marco came out of hiding.

After making certain no one saw him, he opened the bedroom door he knew Francisco never locked and slipped quietly inside, locking the door behind him.

THIRTY-SIX

SUNDAY, MAY 3

Freddy and Francisco settled into the solarium.

Heavy cumulus clouds shielded the warm summer sun and were accompanied by a hearty breeze that brought with it the promise of rain.

Gulls chattered on the bay. A lone squirrel stood impudently in the garden, breakfasting on a pilfered fig.

Freddy's plate was piled high with every conceivable delicacy.

Francisco had a cup of fruit, a dish of yogurt, and a potful of Mexican coffee.

"There's news," Freddy said.

Francisco listened.

"Ricardo has reported there was nothing unusual contained in Kara's cell phone records or on her computer."

"Meaning?"

"She used neither in an incriminating manner."

"Which is good."

"But not definitive."

"Shouldn't this put her in the clear?"

"It's a step in the right direction. We'll know more once we have the opportunity to interview Wanda Ugly."

Francisco smiled.

"So what do we do?"

"We stay on the safe side. For as long as we're here, we keep her under wraps."

"Which means?"

"She's free to do as she pleases, but only in the company of a security detail."

Francisco nodded. "Esteban Marco?"

"No longer in our employ."

"What other news?"

"Your Dodgers lost."

"They're not *my* Dodgers."

"Lucky you."

"Why do you say that?"

"So you won't be depressed when they collapse again."

"Was there anything else, Freddy?"

"I got some good health news. I don't have AIDS."

"Great news. All the more reason for you to keep your dick in your pants."

"Try not to worry yourself about my dick, okay?"

It was then that the sound of gunshots erupted.

———

Kara heard the door to the suite quietly open and then close.

She listened as the lock was engaged. She knew someone else was in her room.

But before she could react, the intruder leapt upon her and slammed a Glock semi into her ribs.

She gasped and attempted to back away, but the intruder prodded her with the pistol and instructed her to get out of bed.

When she did, she recognized the gunman as the same man who had accosted her on the beach, the man she had kicked and humiliated.

"You," she said.

Esteban Marco glared at her.

"What are you doing here?" Kara asked.

"I'm giving a whore what she deserves."

"How dare you speak to me in this manner? Who do you think you are?"

"Your killer."

She carefully studied this man who now held her at gunpoint. Although he brandished his weapon with conviction, she smelled fear on him.

As she had been trained, she set about disarming him psychologically.

"All right," she said.

"All right what?"

"Kill me."

Marco stared at her questioningly.

"Go ahead. Do it," Kara challenged. "Get it over with. Or were you planning to first entertain yourself with me in other ways?"

The initial chink in his armor surfaced. "What are you talking about?"

"You know exactly what I'm talking about. I excite you, don't I?"

"What?"

"You called me a whore. I bet you'd like me to be your whore, wouldn't you?"

She took a bold step toward him, and he instantly shied away.

"Holding a defenseless whore at gunpoint excites you, doesn't it?" Kara said, stepping closer to him. "You're hard, aren't you? You're thinking about how much you'd like to fuck me."

She suddenly shrugged off her nightgown. It fell to the floor, leaving her standing naked before him.

"Go ahead. Have your way with me. Do it to me. Show me what a man you are."

She watched as he attempted to hold eye contact with her. She saw his tongue flick nervously across his lips. She had him on the ropes.

"Come on," she said, moving closer to him. "I'm ready for you. I want you to do it to me. I want you inside me."

She watched him succumb and lower his gaze to admire her nakedness.

Once she saw him look away, she made her move.

In an instant, repeating the Krav Maga feint she had practiced hundreds of times in the classroom, she spun on her heel and, hurtling herself forward, grabbed hold of his gun barrel with her left hand.

Using her body as leverage, she twisted the gun at a sharp right angle and drove it into his thigh. Marco's finger was trapped in the trigger guard, and as she continued to twist the weapon, his finger broke.

He cried out in pain and dropped the pistol. Kara dove for it.

Marco surprised her by doing the same.

As they both reached for it, the pistol skittered away.

Kara reversed her momentum and leapt at him again, slamming into his abdomen headfirst.

He grunted and fell backward.

She dropped to the floor and grabbed hold of the Glock.

Enraged, Marco rushed her, shrieking at the top of his lungs.

He swung his good hand wildly, catching her on the side of the head, sending her reeling backward.

He emitted a deep growl of hatred, lowered his head, and charged.

Kara had trained with a Glock and was familiar with its operation. She chambered a round, and seconds before he barreled into her, she fired.

The bullet struck the crown of his skull, shattering it and sending bits of bone and matter flying everywhere.

He fell on top of her and lay still.

She struggled to extricate herself from beneath him.

Finally she wrested herself free.

She stood, her naked body drenched with his blood and tissue.

Furious and vengeful, she impulsively fired again, further decimating Marco's head.

She experienced a psychological paralysis. Her body was either unwilling or unable to move. She started to tremble. She stood that way even as she heard the gunshots that blew away the lock on the door of the suite.

She became aware of Francisco and Freddy as they barged into the room.

"Are you hit?" Francisco shouted.

"No. The blood is his."

Freddy knelt beside the body. He felt for a pulse. "He's dead," Freddy announced.

Kara emerged from her momentary stupor and looked around.

She realized she was naked.

She spotted a group of armed men milling about in the doorway, also realizing she was naked.

She shouted out to them. "Get the fuck out of here."

They tripped over themselves backing out of the room.

Kara picked up her nightgown and attempted to cover herself with it.

She glared at Francisco, who stood gaping at her, too stunned to react. He made no move to either cover or comfort her.

She turned to Freddy. "I hold you responsible for this," she snarled.

"What are you talking about?"

"You. This is all your doing. I started thinking about you. The confiscation of my phone. My computer. My being held incommunicado. I thought, who was responsible for that? Who gave that order? I knew it couldn't have been Francisco. It could only have been you. You, Freddy. This is all because of you."

Freddy stared at her, then looked away.

She moved closer to him. "You threw down a stink on me, Freddy. Everyone smelled it. Security smelled it. Francisco smelled it. The old man smelled it. The dirtbag lying dead on the floor smelled it. Why, Freddy? Why did you do it?"

Without warning, she slapped his face, staining it with the dead man's blood. "I'll tell you why. You couldn't handle the fact I had usurped some of your position with Francisco. Robbed you of some of your precious closeness. You were gunning for me. Something took place when the riots started, and you pinned it on me. You got Francisco all riled. You undermined our relationship."

She looked pointedly at Francisco, then back at Freddy. "You have no proof of anything. If there was proof, you would already have found it. But you haven't. Because there isn't any. I don't know what you think I've done, but whatever it is, you're dead fucking wrong."

She slapped him again. Harder.

"Get out of here, Freddy," she barked. "Take your hideous costumes and your blatant insecurities and get out of my sight."

Freddy stepped away from her but remained in the room.

Kara turned to Francisco. "If it's all the same to you, I'd like to go home."

She took a deep breath, turned on her heel, and walked into the bathroom, slamming the door behind her.

Freddy turned to Francisco. "You believe her?"

"I love her."

Freddy stared at him. Tears formed in his eyes. He walked slowly to the door.

He looked back at Francisco, who, in turn, looked away.

Then Freddy Sunday scurried downstairs and fled the compound.

THIRTY-SEVEN

Kara stood in the steaming hot shower, watching the water turn from bright red to clear as it cascaded off her body and raced down the drain.

She had taken a calculated risk by challenging Freddy. But she knew if she hadn't been marched out and shot by now, more than likely they couldn't prove her involvement.

She had been flying net-free until the Esteban Marco incident offered her an opportunity to vindicate herself. Being attacked in her rooms was inexcusable, a shocking failure of security. Her indignation was justifiable.

She hoped that by railing against Freddy, she might be able to seize control of the moment and force a reconsideration of her situation.

Informing Francisco she wanted to return to Los Angeles not only raised questions regarding the status of their relationship but also presented a challenge to his authority. She was anxious to see if he took the bait.

In the meantime, she was still being held captive, and if anything incriminating surfaced regarding her involvement in the leaking of Reyes secrets, she would once again find herself under a death threat.

She was determined to keep up the pressure on Francisco to release her and allow her to return home.

She turned off the water, grabbed a towel, and stepped out of the shower.

She found Francisco seated on the commode, staring at her.

"Since when don't you knock?" she said, toweling herself off.

"I did. You didn't hear me."

"You could have waited until I was finished."

"I could have, but I didn't. You were very hard on him."

"Oh, and he wasn't hard on me? It isn't him who's under house arrest."

"I would hardly call it house arrest."

"What would you call it?"

"A retreat."

"A retreat from what? Summer in Los Angeles?"

"From the unpleasantness there. From the widespread rioting and upheaval. We came here to escape any danger."

"That's bullshit, and you know it."

"We came here for our well-being."

"Fuck you, Frankie. You're lying."

"I don't like it when you call me Frankie."

"Tough. Put me on a plane."

"You're overreacting, Kara."

"Overreacting? What are you, blind? I'm being held against my will. I'm followed everywhere by armed guards. I can't use my phone or my computer. On top of which, one of your cherished security bozos nearly killed me in our bed. Overreacting, am I?"

"Please, Kara…"

"No, you please. The facts are the facts. You came to our bed on Friday and treated me like I was distasteful to you. Do you think I didn't notice? How do you think it made me feel?"

"I'm sorry."

"Why don't you take some sincerity lessons, Frankie?"

"What do you want?"

"I want to go back to LA."

"I'm not yet finished with my business here. I'm not ready to leave."

"Then I'll leave without you. There's a noon plane to Phoenix every day. I'll make my way back to LA from there."

"I'm sorry, Kara. I cannot allow that."

"Because you don't trust me."

"I didn't say that."

"Then why?"

"Our operations have been compromised. We are uncertain as to how and why. For now, it's imperative we maintain the highest level of security. Once we are able to stand down and we learn the root of the threat, things will change. Until then we stay where we are."

"So I continue to be your prisoner, is that it?"

"Please don't put it that way."

"What way would you have me put it? Freddy believes I'm the problem. And anything Freddy believes, you believe. Isn't that so?"

Francisco looked away from her.

"Please have me moved to another room. One without you in it. All that remains in this room is the smell of death and the memory of a man I once loved."

He slowly stood and, crestfallen, glanced at her longingly.

Then he exited the bathroom, the suite, and in short order, the compound.

THIRTY-EIGHT

Shelley and I resumed our surveillance of the Reyes villa at dawn. Byron Prescott was with us.

We brought sweet rolls and thermos jugs filled with coffee. We sat in the Explorer, not quite awake, but reinvigorated by the caffeine and the sugar.

With the consent of Governor Chavez, Byron had arranged for the servants to have their Sunday off. After preparing a brown bag lunch and the light breakfast we were currently enjoying, the servants hastily fled, leaving behind only the chief butler and a single security guard.

Which presented Byron with the opportunity to play a key role in the tactical plan he had largely conceived.

In the Explorer, we waged a battle with our lassitude, but sometime shortly after eight, the villa gates opened, and Freddy Sunday walked quickly through them.

Shelley fired up the Explorer, pulled away from the curb, turned right at the corner, and trailed him. She didn't have far to go.

He was two short blocks from the Reyes compound when he entered the grounds of a handsomely restored, lovingly maintained, nineteenth-century hacienda.

He pushed open the unlocked gate, crossed the manicured lawn, and climbed the short flight of steps to the porch.

He pulled a set of keys from his pocket, unlocked the door, and went inside.

Shelley kept driving. After another block or so, she made a U-turn, inched us back to the hacienda, and parked several yards from the entrance gate. She turned off the engine, and the three of us settled in to keep watch.

We finished our coffee and sweet rolls.

"So, what's next?" Shelley asked.

"Hopefully lunch."

"Be serious, Buddy."

"Byron's confident our strategy will deliver the results as planned."

Shelley and I both stared at him.

"It's a sure thing," Byron interjected. "You worry about your part and don't go all batshit about mine."

"A pretty heady statement coming from a confirmed desk jockey."

"I'm totally ready. My materials have been tested and retested. You two bozos should be as prepared as I am."

"And assuming we are?"

"Then I'm trusting your team will arrive as promised."

"They will."

"Are you still maintaining your so-called 'privileged secrecy'?"

"I am."

"Why? Why are you being so secretive?"

"'Cause I don't want to jinx anything."

"And you think by discussing it with us, you'll jinx it?" Byron exclaimed.

"You have to allow me my idiosyncrasies," I said.

"What if we don't pull it off?"

"Getting cold feet, are you, Byron?" Shelley jibed.

"Not in the least. Are you?" Byron retorted.

"I don't want to even think about it." she said.

"But it's a possibility?" Byron asked.

"Snow in July is also a possibility," I said.

"But unlikely."

"Correct."

"I still don't understand how you can be so certain."

"It's a gift." I told him.

THIRTY-NINE

When Kara arrived in the dining room, she discovered Paco José seated at the head of the table. His breakfast had gone largely uneaten. The weakened old man sat staring into space. When she pulled out her chair, he looked up at her.

"Forgive me," he said.

"For what?"

"For not standing."

"There is no need," she said as she sat.

"I hear a great deal of commotion taking place in my house. Even the sound of gunfire. What's happening here that no one has thought to tell me about?"

"There was an incident."

"What kind of incident?"

"Do you remember the man with whom I had the trouble yesterday?"

"I instructed Francisco to get rid of that man."

"He attacked me."

"In my house?"

"He broke into my room and tried to kill me."

"That's inexcusable. Has he been apprehended?"

"He's dead."

"Dead?"

"I shot him."

"You?"

"With his pistol."

"You shot him with his own pistol?"

She nodded.

"And he's dead?"

"Yes."

"Shameful," the old man shrugged. "Have the police been notified?"

"I wouldn't know."

"Where are Freddy and Francisco?"

"Freddy is gone. I have no idea where Francisco might be."

"Freddy is gone?"

"He is."

"Why?"

"There was some sort of security breach at the Reyes offices in Century City. Freddy believes I'm responsible for it."

"Are you?"

"Do you think I would betray your family?"

The old man shook his head.

"I have asked Francisco to allow me to leave. I wish to return to Los Angeles."

"And?"

"He has refused me."

"Because?"

"He no longer trusts me."

"There is unpleasantness between you?"

"There is. Will you help me?"

"Help you?"

"Yes."

"Help you how?"

"Help me leave here."

The old man sat silently for the longest while.

Then he slowly raised himself out of his chair. "I cannot intervene in Francisco's affairs."

"Even when they're unjust?"

"That is not for me to determine."

"I don't understand. You are the Don."

"Francisco is the Don. I am not well, Kara. I am no longer concerned with the occurrences of life. I am preparing myself for death."

"But you are still alive, Paco. You are still a wise and just man."

"Enough. Basta. I have given you my answer." He turned from the table and began to shuffle away.

"I'm fighting for my life too," she said.

"You are greatly tiring me, Kara."

"You're a hypocrite. I would never have guessed it."

"And you are under suspicion. I would never have guessed that."

"I am innocent until proven guilty. That's the American way."

The old man forced a chuckle. "You are guilty until proven innocent. That's the Paco way."

Kara watched as he slowly left the room.

FORTY

Francisco burst through the gates of the compound as if he was on fire.

He looked neither left nor right as he made a beeline for Freddy's hacienda.

After several moments, a black Mercedes sedan roared through the gates and followed him.

Francisco slowed when he reached Freddy's hacienda. He made his way to the house and knocked several times on the door.

There was no response. He rang the bell.

Still no response.

Enervated, he walked slowly to the gate, and once there, looked forlornly back at the hacienda.

Then he stepped into the Mercedes that had followed him.

The three of us watched this from inside the Explorer, which was parked within sight of the hacienda.

"Let's move," I said. "Let's beat him there."

"To the church?" Shelley asked.

"As planned."

Shelley swung into action.

As she drove, I commented, "The Church of Our Lady of

Guadalupe. It thrives as a result of Francisco's funding. He visits every Sunday he's in Puerto Peñasco."

We arrived at the church in what had to be record time, exited the Explorer, and took up our respective posts.

The church is more than a century old, a stone and mortar edifice, superbly maintained, situated on a seemingly boundless plot of what had once been wasteland.

Behind the church sprawls an ancient cemetery, home to a vast array of tombstones, monuments, and shrines, many as old as the church itself.

It was an overcast morning with the threat of rain in the air, which reduced the normal Sunday crowds to a minimum.

We drove slowly along the unpaved roadway and located the whereabouts of the Reyes memorial plot.

We parked nearby.

We were examining a pair of eighteenth-century archangel statues designed by Miguel Mateo Cabrera, who, during his lifetime, was recognized as Mexico's greatest artist, when we saw Francisco arrive.

The driver parked the Mercedes in the church lot, adjacent to where an ancient crone was hawking nosegays and bouquets of various colorful flowers.

Francisco greeted her with extended arms. They hugged for several moments.

Following a brief conversation, Francisco pressed several bills into her trembling hand and received a blossoming spray of red and yellow roses in exchange.

One of the two bodyguards who had accompanied Francisco stood apart from him, watching the exchange.

Francisco nodded to him and headed for his mother's burial plot, where he dropped to his knees, placed the flowers in front of her ornate headstone, and silently engaged in ardent prayer.

Byron and I moved swiftly to Francisco's side.

I was holding the chloroform-treated washcloth Byron had provided. Legend has it the dense, colorless, and strong-smelling liquid has been repeatedly used by criminals to knock out, daze, and even murder their prey.

Contrary to popular belief, however, while chloroform is a powerful sedative, it takes several minutes for it to render a person unconscious.

Having carefully plotted our attack, Byron now captained it.

Startled by our encroaching proximity, Francisco leapt to his feet.

Glancing at us, and quickly sizing each of us up, his initial instinct was to rail first against Byron.

After hollering to his bodyguard, Francisco turned toward Byron, who quickly plastered him with a shot from the stun gun he was brandishing.

As he staggered off-balance, I moved behind Francisco and wrapped my arms around his neck and shoulders, slamming the chloroform-doused washrag onto his mouth and nose.

Together with Byron, I propped Francisco up, holding him steady, waiting for the powerful chemical to render him unconscious.

But having witnessed our onslaught, Francisco's bodyguard, who had been lounging nearby, sprang into action.

Or, rather, he attempted to spring into action. He was prevented from so doing by Shelley Hartman, who had surreptitiously maneuvered herself close to him.

It was the first shot from Hartman's Taser that staggered the bodyguard.

The second one knocked him off his feet.

He dropped to the ground, jerking and convulsing.

Shelley silenced him by slamming the heel of the stun gun into the side of his head.

Then she doubled back and Tasered the second bodyguard, who was seated behind the wheel of the Mercedes, and who never saw it coming.

Meanwhile, Francisco was recovering from the Taser shot, but had not yet been rendered unconscious by the chloroform.

Shaken and somewhat woozy, he nonetheless lashed out.

He was clinging to both Byron and me when he altered his weight distribution and landed a hard kick to Byron's crotch.

Now staggering himself, Byron let go of his hold on Francisco.

Although I was suddenly bearing his full weight, I was still able to continue thrusting the washrag forcefully into Francisco's face.

Floundering, Francisco made every effort to wrest himself from my grasp.

He was a big man, agile and strong.

He managed to elbow me in the ribs, which caused me to relax my hold on him slightly.

He elbowed me again, and in an instant, did it once more.

Rattled by his attack, I was forced to release my grip on him.

Although still groggy, the big man began pummeling me with his fists.

Byron, on the ground nearby, was struggling to regain his footing.

Francisco took notice of him. His attention was captured by the stun gun in Byron's hand.

He reached out and violently snatched it.

He was toying with the stun gun when I stepped up to him and landed a sharp right to his cheek.

Already staggering, the blow decked Francisco. He fell heavily.

I jumped on him and once again slammed the chloroformed washrag onto his nose and mouth.

I held tight to both the washrag and Francisco.

We stayed that way for a couple of minutes.

I could feel Francisco's resistance begin to wane.

Finally he slipped into unconsciousness.

Byron stood watching us.

"Shelley," I said.

He nodded and headed toward where he had last spotted her and the bodyguards.

The first bodyguard was still unconscious on the ground.

"The driver?" he asked Shelley.

"Resting comfortably," she replied and then asked, "Francisco?"

"Dreamland."

"Maybe it's time we blew this joint," Shelley posited.

"Works for me," Byron said.

Byron helped me hoist Francisco to his feet and load him into the Wrangler.

Within seconds Shelley was behind the wheel, and we were on our way.

FORTY-ONE

The driveway gate at the rear of the governor's mansion opened, the Explorer entered, and the gate slid closed.

Byron was the first one out of the big Ford, and he pointed Shelley to a parking place behind the main house.

Then he ushered the security guard away from the gatehouse and its vantage point of the Explorer.

Once we were out of view, I lifted Francisco from his seat and together with Shelley, escorted him into the mansion.

He was still suffering the effects of the chloroform and offered no resistance.

We dropped him on top of the queen-sized brass bed in Byron's room. I cuffed his hands to a pair of headposts. Then I cuffed his feet to the footposts.

Francisco stirred, but then fell back into his drug-induced stupor.

Byron joined us in the bedroom. We spoke softly, waiting for Francisco to awaken.

"Have you heard from the team?" he asked.

"They'll be arriving on schedule."

"Looks like Francisco's coming around," Shelley said.

"He'll be disoriented for a while," I said.

"Welcome to the club," Byron joked.

Francisco groaned. He attempted to move his hands and feet. His eyes fluttered open. He looked around.

The unfamiliar surroundings alarmed him. He began to thrash about in an effort to free himself of his constraints. His eyes widened with fear. "Who are you?" he asked.

"Friends of Kara."

"Kara?"

"Surely you remember Kara."

Francisco glared at me. "What do you want from me?"

"We're going to trade you."

"Trade me? For Kara?"

"Yep"

"It'll never work," he stammered. "Freddy will never make such a trade."

"Try to understand me, Francisco," I said. "We're going to make a one-time offer. One that Freddy dare not refuse. We'll make our demands, and he will have a limited amount of time in which to meet them. If he fails to respond on a timely basis, we start lopping off your fingers until he does."

"Lopping off my fingers? My fingers? What kind of people are you?"

"The same kind as you," I said.

FORTY-TWO

It had become apparent to those in the compound that something was awry.

Having had time to cool off, Freddy returned to the villa in search of Francisco.

Francisco's bodyguards preceded him. They informed Freddy that Francisco had been taken.

A sudden chill crept up Freddy's spine.

The bodyguards were red-faced with shame. They had no idea where he was.

Freddy was livid.

He summoned the captain of the guards and ordered him to eliminate the two bodyguards. They were to blame for what happened to Francisco. They deserved to pay for it with their lives.

Freddy considered every possible scenario.

Then it dawned on him that Francisco was going to be traded for Kara.

———

I returned to the bedroom where Francisco was being held.

He yelled at me. "Where were you? Why has no one come to check on me? Where am I?"

"Which answer do you want first?"

"I have to pee."

"I'm not stopping you."

"In the toilet."

"Oh, in the toilet."

Francisco glared at me.

I took the keys from my pocket and removed the cuff from the left side of the footpost and secured it to Francisco's right foot, thereby binding his feet together.

Then I recuffed his hands in front of him and stepped away from the bed.

I produced my Colt semi and trained it on him. "Okay. The bathroom's over there."

"I can't walk with my feet bound."

"Hop."

"Excuse me?"

"Hop to the toilet. And do it quickly."

Francisco awkwardly hopped his way to the bathroom. Then he reached back as if to close the door behind him.

"Leave it open."

"I can't pee when someone's watching."

"Get over it."

When I heard the flush, I called out "Now hop back."

After a moment, Francisco appeared in the doorway, hopping toward the bed.

All of a sudden he leapt at me. The heavy metal handcuffs caught me just above my left ear but without enough force to do any damage.

The leap caused Francisco to lose his balance. He fell heavily to his knees.

I then slammed the butt handle of my pistol into the side of his face.

He toppled over. Blood appeared on his cheek.

I yanked him to his feet and literally threw him onto the bed.

I then resecured his cuffed hands and feet to the bed.

"You don't learn your lesson, do you?" I said. "That was pretty stupid."

"I'm bleeding."

"How awful for you."

"What are you going to do about it?"

"How about nothing."

"You mean you'd let me just lie here bleeding?"

"Pretty much."

"You'll pay for this."

"You think?"

I stepped to the bed and smacked him in the mouth with the flat of my hand. "Don't underestimate me, Francisco."

Then I turned and walked to the door.

"Wait," he said.

I turned back to him.

"I need a doctor."

"What planet do you live on? You're a prisoner who attacked his captor. And now you want medical attention? Is there something I'm missing here?"

Francisco glared at me.

"You made your own bed, pal. Now you can bleed in it."

FORTY-THREE

Kara sensed still yet another change in the mood of the compound.

Her interest had been piqued when Freddy inquired as to Francisco's whereabouts. It was highly unlikely he could have fallen off the radar, because his movements were usually so predictable.

Although Francisco and Freddy had argued fiercely, that wouldn't have prevented Francisco from making his ritualistic Sunday morning visit to the Church of Our Lady of Guadalupe.

It was also unlike him to venture any distance from the villa without being accompanied by armed bodyguards.

She crept downstairs to see if she could learn more. The house was abuzz with activity, and to Kara's eye, it was more chaotic than usual.

She ventured into the butler's pantry and there ran across Patricia Navarro, the assistant housekeeper.

She closed the door behind her. "Patricia?"

"*Sí*, Kara."

"What's all the commotion?"

"Surely you must know."

"Know what?"

"Señor Francisco has been taken."

"Taken?"

"*Sí*. No one knows where he is."

Patricia lowered her voice to a whisper. "Maria Loza claims she overheard Freddy saying something about a trade."

"A trade?"

"Shush. *Sí*," Patricia said, holding her finger to her lips. "Him for you."

Kara was stunned. "A trade for me?"

"According to Maria Loza."

Kara thanked Patricia for sharing her information.

She wandered back to her room.

"A trade," she murmured to herself.

Then, after a moment, she whispered, "Buddy."

FORTY-FOUR

At approximately three p.m., a sleek C-20 superjet, the military version of the Gulfstream G 4, taxied to a stop at the Aerodromo Internacional Puerto Peñasco, the small, private airport located on the outer edges of town.

Adapted for military use, the C-20 is primarily employed for command and executive transport. It has been configured to seat eight and accommodate a crew of three.

The hydraulically operated staircase deployed, and once secured, three passengers deplaned, each wearing nondescript khaki pants and shirts, each carrying an operations duffel packed with the weaponry and other equipment that their mission required.

Awaiting them on the tarmac was Governor Ignacio Chavez, accompanied by a single immigration officer, who officially admitted the men to Mexico.

Each of the passengers shook hands with the governor and the officer, following which both officials hurriedly climbed into the governor's waiting limousine and sped away.

The three arrivals took note of the Ford Explorer parked nearby.

The leader of the group, Lieutenant Colonel Darwin O'Conner, known to all as "Doc," wandered over to the Explorer and acknowledged its driver, who was leaning against the front fender, watching the new arrivals out of heavy-lidded eyes.

The two others followed in close order, each of them giving the driver the once-over, each of them shaking his head as though in disappointment.

"This has to be the biggest blunder of my career," Doc said.

"Will you just look at this bozo," Major Dustin "Dusty" Stengel said, pointing to the driver.

"Doesn't the LAPD have any kind of conditioning requirements?" Captain Peter Brigham said.

"I wonder if it's too late to get back on the plane," Doc mused.

I lifted myself off the Explorer's fender and regarded the three men. "You ask for elite, they send the Three Stooges."

"Nyuk, nyuk," Doc said.

I stepped over to him. We regarded each other warily.

"Butt ugly," Doc said.

"Ditto."

Then Doc reached over and gathered me into a hearty bear hug. "But you're definitely a welcome sight."

I grinned.

The other men gathered around. A great deal of back-slapping, insulting, and laughter ensued.

Then we all bundled ourselves into the Explorer and pulled away from the airport, just as the C-20 lifted off for its return flight.

———

I had contacted Doc O'Conner when Kara was spirited off to Puerto Peñasco.

Doc, who had been my superior officer in Los Angeles, had returned to his military roots and was currently in service at Camp Pendleton, in Oceanside, California, eighty or so miles south of LA.

O'Conner had tried his damnedest to convince me to rejoin him in the Marines. We had worked side by side in LA, training young recruits by day and carousing by night. We became fast friends.

Although only a couple of years my senior, O'Conner had risen quickly through the ranks and was now a junior member of the Marine Corps command group, wherein expectations for him were high.

We had remained in close contact, and after Doc transferred to Pendleton, we were able to occasionally grab some downtime together, hiking, golfing, and carousing.

When the Francisco Reyes adventure morphed into a rescue mission, I sought Doc's advice. He had surprised me by suggesting he might be able to assist.

In virtually no time, he had outlined a plan and presented it to me. I agreed to it on the spot.

That initiated a chain of events that also found Dusty and Pete hurriedly on their way to Oceanside to join in.

Those three men comprised one of the Marine Corps' elite groups of training instructors. Over the course of several years, they sent hundreds of well-prepared servicemen and women into the wilds of foreign territories, many of them to instruct other young soldiers, much like they did.

I had been among their number for my entire stay in the Corps, first as a trainee, then as a valued member of the training team.

The four of us had been inseparable. We lived together in the leadership barracks. We were exceptionally diligent and worked tirelessly to mold raw recruits into a solidly trained force.

When we weren't working, however, we were playing with the same degree of dedication we brought to the work.

Many was the time we staggered onto base barely in time for reveille.

But even in a debauched state, our work ethic and our standards had never been compromised.

Now we were reunited. Five years later.

For one more mission.

FORTY-FIVE

Freddy had requested a meeting with Paco José, and the old man had granted the request on the condition that the meeting be held in his quarters. This wasn't one of his better days, and he was unable to muster enough strength to make his way downstairs.

When Freddy entered his room, he was taken aback by how much the old man had deteriorated. He was lying in a hospital bed, the mattress adjusted so the Don could sit upright.

His weight loss was considerable. He was exceptionally frail. But his mind was still sharp, and his attention was focused. "What brings you to my bedside?"

"Forgive me, Don Paco, it wasn't my wish to disturb you."

"I understand. How may I be of service?"

"There has been an incident."

"So many incidents. What now?"

"Francisco has been taken."

"Taken?"

"Kidnapped."

"How could this be?"

"I'm not certain."

"But you believe he was kidnapped."

"Yes."

"By whom?"

Freddy evaded the old man's gaze and didn't respond to his question.

"You are uncomfortable," Don Paco observed.

"Yes."

"This has something to do with the situation in Los Angeles?"

"I believe so."

"Involving Kara?"

"It would appear as if Francisco was taken so he might then be exchanged for her."

"So she was the one?"

"It's likely."

"What is it you want?"

"I want Francisco back."

"Have any demands been made known?"

"Not yet."

"But you believe they will be."

"Yes. And soon. They will want this matter resolved quickly."

"They being?"

"I'm guessing the LAPD."

"And they will return Francisco in exchange for Kara?"

"Likely so."

"And when will this alleged trade be made?"

"That's why I'm here."

"To discuss with me your plan?"

"Yes."

The Don was silent. After a while he spoke again. "Am I to assume you have something up your sleeve?"

"I have an idea."

"And you have come to tell me about it."

"Yes."

"I'm all ears," Paco José said.

FORTY-SIX

Puerto Peñasco cherished its public park, dedicated to and donated by Paco Luis Reyes in the name of his family.

Reyes Park was a haven for the locals, acres of open fields devoted to sports, recreational facilities, playgrounds, and activities for children.

The three Marines and I studiously reconnoitered the park in search of strategic locations suitable for our needs.

We took measurements. We studied sight lines and trajectory arcs. We discussed the pros and cons of every conceivable vantage point.

After completing our inspection, we piled back into the Explorer and returned to the hacienda.

Byron had arranged for us to have a sumptuous Mexican feast.

Homemade guacamole and freshly prepared salads were in abundance. Ceviche, shrimp, and calamari rested on beds of freshly shaved ice. Steaming plates of chicken, beef, and pork enchiladas sat beside ample servings of Mexican rice and refried beans.

Fresh corn and flour tortillas were laid out next to bowls of corn chips and a sampling of various salsas, ranging from mild to set-the-roof-of-your-mouth-on-fire.

There were urns filled with Mexican coffee and tubs of ice filled with bottles of beer.

The three Marines circled the table like tigers in search of prey.

Then they turned their attention to Byron.

I had a pretty good idea where this was going. I stood back to enjoy it.

"Big disappointment," Major Dusty Stengel said to him. "How could Buddy not have told you I keep kosher?"

"And I'm vegan," Captain Petey Brigham added.

"Is there a Chinese takeout in the neighborhood?" Doc asked. "I don't much care for Mexican."

Byron was in shock. "Chinese?"

"Don't pay any attention to these morons," I said. "They're pulling your chain."

"I thought this was a good meal," Byron said.

"Read my lips, Byron," Shelley said. "They're teasing you."

Byron looked around.

Doc O'Conner winked at him.

Petey Brigham filled his plate first. Brigham was the prototype of an old-time Marine. He was built like a fireplug, short and stocky. No one could remember a time when he didn't have the mangled remains of a chewed cigar planted in the corner of his mouth. Spitting was his favorite pastime.

He was also a marksmen first class, lethal with a sniper rifle from record distances. He had grown up on a cattle ranch in Montana and was given his first rifle before he was five.

He spent his youth perfecting his skills and increasing his range. He was the state champion while still in junior high school.

Now he designed high-impact, long-range rifles for the military and on occasion, was called upon to make the most difficult kill shots—shots that other marksmen could not achieve.

Dusty Stengel was the resident expert in SMAW, Shoulder-Launched Multipurpose Assault Weapons. An 83mm, man-portable rocket launcher, the SMAW was a modernized version of the old-fashioned bazooka.

A tall, leathery, beanpole of a man, Dusty helped replace the original rifle-aiming system with a new, bore-sighting system, thereby making the weapon quicker and more accurate.

Doc O'Conner had early on seen the potential in these men and had purposefully recruited each of them. He shared the secrets of proper training procedures with them and drilled them until they became masters.

Then he molded them into the Marine equivalent of an educational dream team.

After stuffing themselves on Byron's feast, the Marines settled down to once again check and recheck their equipment, which included a quartet of M-40, A One precision sniper rifles, each hand-tooled by USMC armorers, as well as the latest version of the SMAW rocket launcher, developed by the engineers at McDonnell Douglas under the supervision of Dusty Stengel.

They inspected sights and night scopes, optics and stands. They double-checked magazines and loads.

Then, one by one, they returned to the buffet table to further browse the desserts.

FORTY-SEVEN

At four o'clock, I phoned Paco José Reyes at his compound.

It took several minutes to be connected to the old man, who spoke in a raspy voice, which impressed me as being tired and freighted.

"We are holding your son," I told the old man. "We are willing to exchange him for Kara Machado."

"Say her name again."

"Please don't trivialize this, Señor Reyes. If you wish to be reunited with Francisco, you will need to be standing by the phone at ten o'clock this evening. You will then be given instructions as to the time and place of the proposed exchange."

"I will make myself available at that time. But I must inform you that I am bedridden and physically incapable of participating in any exchange."

"You may name a surrogate. Assuming the surrogate is acceptable to us."

"I will appoint Federico Domingo."

"Freddy Sunday?"

"Yes."

"He'll do. I will expect both of you to be on the ten o'clock call."

Before the Don could respond, I ended the call.

In his bedroom, the old man looked at Freddy, who was seated beside him. "You were correct."

"So far, so good," Freddy said.

———

Doc O'Conner and I sat on beach chairs on the waterfront terrace, watching the sun dip in and out of the increasingly cloudy late-afternoon sky and listening to the screeching of the gulls.

"So, tell me the real reason," I said.

"The real reason for what?"

"I know you didn't reassemble this team for sentimental value. You don't get to play with all these government-owned toys just to exercise your mojo."

"So young yet so cynical."

"Come on, Doc. Don't fuck with a fucker."

"We have an interest in the Pacos."

"Meaning?"

"The Feds are none too thrilled by the prospect of the streets of Los Angeles suddenly bursting with high-end crystal meth. The activities of the cartels are on the rise. The home team believes it's time to deal them a blow."

"So your interest isn't solely rescuing a damsel in distress?"

"Not solely."

"Was it really the Feds who called in the Marines?"

"That's what they do when they feel the temperature rising."

"And the damsel thing?"

"The perfect wave to ride in on. When the riots postponed the meth drop, we realized the drugs needed to be stored some-where. They were packed and ready to ship, but now they had to be warehoused until the shitstorm passed and LA was once again open for business."

"So?"

"We have reason to believe it's in the Reyes compound."

"Here?"

Doc nodded.

"Why would they bring it here?"

"They had to bring it somewhere."

"But to their compound?"

"We think they may have created a red herring."

"Meaning?"

"They made it appear as if they had housed the stash in a storage facility just south of Nogales. They used that facility for drop storage before. They stationed a cadre of armed guards around the facility to lend credence to the ruse."

"So why would they then stash them here?"

"These drugs have an exceptionally high street value. They promise to be one of the largest scores ever for the Pacos. But because the riots suddenly unsettled everything, we believe they became uncertain as to just how long the meth would have to remain in storage. And where. They figured the red herring would throw any interested dogs off the actual scent. For the moment. Bringing them home was their safest bet. We suspect Francisco Reyes did just that."

"Let me guess. You'd like to chat with him about this."

"Dusty and I would very much appreciate the chance to talk with Señor Francisco. It would give us the opportunity to con- firm our suppositions."

"And if he clams up?"

"He won't."

"How do you know?"

"We're fairly confident he'll respond to carefully applied pressure."

"Meaning?"

"Don't ask."

"When would you like to have this chat?"

"As my mama used to say, 'Ain't no time like the now.'"

———

"You'll captain the ship," I reiterated to Byron. "Shelley will coordinate the transport efforts. She'll pick you up in the Explorer. You should be able to make the crossing by dawn."

We were seated on the veranda, facing the sea. The late afternoon sun was a ball of fire in the sky as it sank lower on the horizon. The air was ripe with the pungent smell of wood-burning beach fires. We could hear the distant sound of children's laughter.

"Once we're gone," I instructed, "pack the remaining gear and wipe everything down. It's important you be on the road before the shit hits the fan."

"The new car will be in San Luis Rio Colorado?" Shelley asked.

"At the same place we picked up the Explorer. Keys on the driver's side rear wheel. Clean any prints in or on the Explorer, change vehicles, and you're good to go."

"What could go wrong?" Byron asked.

"You'd be surprised," Doc O'Conner said as he stepped onto the veranda. "We've already got a change of plan. Our good buddy Francisco confirmed the meth is stashed in the compound. In the Paco Luis house."

"So what's the change of plan?"

"We're going to eradicate the stash."

"In the compound?"

"Exactly."

FORTY-EIGHT

I made the ten o'clock call and was immediately connected to Freddy Sunday and Paco José Reyes. "You will be phoned again at midnight with the instructions."

"Midnight?" Freddy said. "Why not now?"

"Midnight," I said and hung up.

I looked around at the others in the room. Doc and his team were there. As were Shelley and Byron. "Are we ready?"

Doc nodded. "Let's do it."

Shelley grabbed a duffel and headed for the Explorer, followed closely by Petey Brigham, who also carried a gear bag. They quickly loaded up, climbed in, and drove off.

Shelley made her way through the deserted streets of Puerto Peñasco, stopping only at Reyes Park, where she dropped Petey.

Waving to her, he grabbed his duffel, spat out a mouthful of foul-smelling tobacco, and disappeared into the darkness of the park.

Shelley then returned to the governor's house.

———

Kara was confined to her room. There were two armed guards in front of her door, and if she wished to go anywhere in the compound, she would either be accompanied by them or denied the privilege.

She was lying on her bed, staring at the ceiling, when the door opened, and Freddy Sunday entered.

She glared at him. "How dare you burst into my room like this."

"I'm so sorry. Did I offend your delicate sensibilities?"

"Don't fuck with me, Freddy. What do you want?"

"I'm going to prepare you."

"Prepare me for what?"

"You're about to find out."

———

When Shelley got back, Dusty Stengel and Doc O'Conner loaded their equipment into the Explorer.

Then they reconnoitered the house in search of anything that might have been left behind.

Doc sought me out. I was assisting in Byron's cleanup mission. "We're good to go," he said.

I gazed at my watch. It was nearing eleven thirty. "Francisco?"

"Dusty's preparing him. I heard you made detective."

"Looks like it."

"I presume congratulations are in order."

"If you say so."

Doc smiled. "I say so. Nice going, Buddy."

I shrugged.

Doc looked at his watch.

"How long?" I asked.

"Five minutes maybe."

"We'll meet in the great room in five minutes."

Doc nodded and headed for the door.

"Doc," I called to him.

He turned to me.

"Thanks," I said.

Doc flashed the peace sign, then left the room.

———

Freddy carefully selected Kara's wardrobe. He pored through the closet searching for just the right outfit.

She watched him. "What are you doing?"

"I want you to look your best."

"For what?"

"For Francisco."

"I thought you said he was taken."

"He was."

"I don't understand."

"Trust me. You need to look great."

"For the trade?"

"Excuse me?"

"Don't play dumb with me, Freddy. Everybody knows about it."

"All the more reason for you to look your best."

"I'll look the way I want to look."

"You'll look as I tell you to look."

"Fuck you, Freddy. I'll wear what I want."

Freddy stepped over to her and slapped her face.

"Your physical condition isn't a part of the deal. You may think you can wear whatever you want, but if you defy me and my choices, you'll be in a fair amount of pain at trade time. *Comprende?*"

She glared at him.

He turned his attention back to her closet.

He chose a low-cut sleeveless black dress, as well as a pair of high-heeled shoes. He handed them to her. "Put these on."

She looked at him and did nothing.

Then he pushed her backward and shouted at her, "Do it."

She picked up the clothing and stepped into the bathroom to change in private.

"Makeup," he said.

"Excuse me?"

"Don't forget the makeup."

She closed the bathroom door behind her.

Freddy grinned.

He had chosen the perfect outfit for her to die in.

———

At eleven thirty, Shelley, Doc, Byron, and I gathered in the great room.

We heard Dusty before he actually appeared. He was leading Francisco, who was blindfolded and gagged, his hands tethered tightly behind him. His feet were bound together, but loosely enough to allow him to shuffle.

He attempted to speak through his gag but was immediately silenced by Dusty, who smacked him in the back of the head. "No talking."

I noticed additional bruising on one of Francisco's cheeks.

"What happened?"

"Carefully applied pressure," Doc said. He looked at his watch. "Eleven forty."

"Post time," I said. Byron smiled.

We high-fived.

Then Shelley and I left the governor's house and headed for

the Explorer, followed by Dusty and Doc, with Francisco shuffling along between them.

———

Freddy grabbed Kara by the arm and pushed her roughly through the door and down the stairs.

No guards were present, and the house was inordinately quiet.

Freddy escorted her to Paco José's quarters.

The old man was sitting in a mechanized wheelchair.

A metal table lay across the arms of the chair. On it sat a pitcher of water, a drinking glass, and several vials filled with pills. The Don had on a silk dressing gown worn over a pair of cotton pajamas.

"We're leaving now," Freddy said. "I thought you might want to say something to her."

Don Paco looked at her. "You betrayed us."

Kara chose not to acknowledge the old man.

"The only mercy you can hope for will be a quick death."

"I wish the same for you," she said.

The old man looked at Freddy. "Get her out of my sight."

Freddy pulled her away and shoved her forcefully out of the room.

FORTY-NINE

MONDAY, MAY 4

At midnight, I phoned the compound. Freddy picked up the call.

"Bring Kara to Reyes Park in half an hour. Twelve thirty sharp. Use the entrance on Calle Santa Catalina, the one leading to the playground. Just the two of you. No one else. Stand in front of the large slide. Francisco and I will join you there. Do you understand the instructions?"

"Yes."

"Good. Don't fuck this up, Freddy. There won't be any second chances."

———

From his vantage point atop the Reyes Park Recreation Center, Petey Brigham saw a Jeep Wrangler turn slowly onto Calle Santa Catalina and approach the entrance to the playground.

The vehicle pulled to a stop, and five men armed with assault rifles climbed out. One by one they crept into the park. The Wrangler drove off.

Petey was wearing night vision goggles, and he witnessed their movements clearly.

Three of the men hurried to the far side of the park and secreted themselves as best they could among concrete benches, pinon trees, and a pair of abundant succulent plants.

The two others remained on the near side, gingerly insinuating themselves behind a cluster of spiny prickly pear cactus, the only viable shelter available.

Petey glanced at his watch. It was several minutes past midnight. He opened his military cell phone and punched in a number.

"Buddy," came the immediate answer.

"Five," Petey said.

"You good to go?"

"*Si, señor,*" he said and ended the call.

Petey examined the precision M-40 sniper rifle once again. He checked the night scope and the silencing mechanism.

He took several deep breaths. Then he removed the cigar butt from his mouth, turned his head, and hocked a loogie over the wall.

———

Doc and I watched as a Volkswagen minibus left the compound.

We were sitting in the Explorer, Shelley and I in front, Doc and Dusty on either side of Francisco in the back. We were parked in the shadows, a short distance from the Reyes compound.

I glanced at my watch. "Right on time."

Dusty and Doc got out of the Explorer.

Dusty stepped to the back of the vehicle, opened the cargo door, and removed two equipment bags.

I lowered his window. "One o'clock," I said.

"One o'clock," Doc echoed.

"And if we're not there?"

"We start without you."

———

Petey watched the Volkswagen minibus pull up in front of the playground gate.

He shouldered his sniper rifle, spat out a wad of phlegm, then stared down the scope and zeroed in on the Volkswagen's left front wheel.

He squeezed off the first round. It hit the tire, which immediately began to deflate.

He focused on the rear tire, which moments later he also flattened.

He lowered the M-40 and raised himself up to see the results, which pleased him.

This time when he spat, he lost control of the cigar butt, and it too flew out of his mouth. His clumsiness made him grin.

The Volkswagen had settled onto the rims of the driver's side wheels and was now listing left. Its balance had been seriously impaired. The sudden shifting of weight threatened its stability.

Tilting dramatically, the minibus was teetering on the verge of falling over.

The driver's side front window slowly lowered, and Freddy's head appeared in it. He looked around, trying to determine whether or not it was safe for him to open the door.

In the back of the minibus, Kara braced herself against the right side of the vehicle, her arms above her head, holding on to the handgrip located just above the window.

Then she launched herself off the right side of the vehicle

and repeatedly used her weight to pummel the already teetering left side.

"What in the fuck," Freddy yelled.

Kara bent her knees and launched another series of kicks. This time she caught the side of the minibus at a moment it was rocking left, and her kick caused it to tip over and fall onto its side.

———

Freddy had narrowly escaped being pinned when the Volkswagen tipped over. He managed to extricate himself from the driver's seat and tentatively stand on it.

Then he launched himself into the rear of the minibus and tackled Kara.

She fell heavily, immobilized in his grasp.

Enraged, he grabbed her foot, wrested off the high-heeled shoe, and savagely twisted her ankle until he heard it snap.

Kara screamed.

"Try kicking now, bitch," Freddy snarled as he released her and inched back into the front of the van.

Kara curled into a ball, nursing her painfully broken foot.

Standing upright on the driver's side door, Freddy reached over and lowered the passenger side window.

He stuck his head out.

Access to the minibus was normally through the two front doors and a pair of barn doors on the left side of the vehicle. With the vehicle now resting on its left side, the passenger side door was its only egress.

Freddy attempted to push the door open, but its weight resisted his effort.

He called out to Kara, instructing her to move to the front of the bus so she could help him get out.

When she refused, he made a move toward her. "Do as I say or I'll break your other foot."

She glared at him and tentatively began making her way to the driver's side.

"Kneel down on the door. I'm going to stand on your back."

"I can't. My foot."

He viciously slapped her face. "Do it!"

She recoiled.

He made a move as if to slap her again.

She raised her hands in an effort to ward off the blow. "Okay, okay," she said.

She gingerly lowered herself onto her knees on the driver's side door.

Freddy climbed onto her back, allowing himself just enough leverage to open the VW's passenger side window.

Then, with his feet planted firmly on her back, he bent his knees slightly and thrust himself upward, through the open window and out of the vehicle.

He looked down and saw her kneeling on the door, whimpering, massaging her broken foot.

"So much for the best-laid plans," he muttered to himself.

FIFTY

"Where exactly are they?" I asked.

"In front of the entrance to the playground," Petey answered.

"And the *soldados*?"

"Just now emerging."

"Doing what?"

"Searching for me."

"Will they find you?"

"You're kidding, right?"

Petey ended the call, squatted down, and picked up the errant cigar butt, dusted it off, put it back in his mouth and clamped down hard on it.

He was double-checking his rifle when he heard a noise behind him. He turned just in time to spot one of the *soldados* clambering onto the rec center roof.

The *soldado* spotted Petey and reached for his pistol. Petey raised his rifle and shot him.

The sound suppressor masked any noise, but the proximity of the *soldado* to the weapon didn't result in a pretty ending. The big M-40 blew right through him, sending bits and pieces of him flying in every direction.

"Shit," Petey said, dodging a barrage of blood and gore, a good deal of which managed to land on him regardless.

He spat, then wet and slimy, he reached into his duffel and pulled out a towel. He dried his face and hands. He cleaned the barrel of his rifle.

"Shit," he said again.

He spat out his cigar butt in disgust.

Then he turned his attention back to the playground entrance.

———

Freddy looked at his watch. Less than ten minutes to go. With no little effort, he lowered himself back into the minibus and reached for his shoulder bag.

He extracted the device from it.

He looked at Kara, who was seated awkwardly on the driver's side door, protecting her foot.

"I have a little gift for you," he said.

"What gift?"

"A charming bracelet. And a necklace, too."

"What are you talking about?"

He took a pair of handcuffs from his bag.

He maneuvered himself into position beside her, and taking hold of her wrist, snapped one of the cuffs onto it. Then he grabbed her other arm, pulled it behind her and cuffed her wrists together.

"Voilà," he said. "The bracelet."

Then he grabbed the device and maneuvered the silver chain on which it was hanging around her neck and secured it with its jewelry clips. The device fell just below her neck.

"What is this?" she asked, her heart sinking as she began to grasp what Freddy was doing.

"A necklace. Charming, no?"

"This is an explosive device?"

"Actually, it's a time bomb. Designed and constructed by our very own team of engineers. Once I activate it, you will have exactly twelve minutes before boom, *adios*."

Kara glared at him.

"You didn't think you'd actually get away with it, did you?" He sneered. "You underestimated us, Kara. Now you'll get to experience the singular thrill of pulverization. And you're dressed perfectly for it too."

"You're insane."

"Am I? Gee, I never thought of it that way. Thanks for the insight."

He glanced at his watch. Then he reached down and pressed a button on the side of the device.

A red light flashed on. The time bomb began to emit a loud, steady ticking sound, much like that of a clock.

"Twelve minutes," he said.

Then he stepped onto her shoulder and launched himself up and out of the Volkswagen.

FIFTY-ONE

Finding no available parking spaces nearby, Shelley double-parked behind the fallen Volkswagen, where Freddy could be seen sitting atop it, a Beretta pistol in his hand.

I got out of the Explorer and approached him. "You," Freddy said.

"Happy to see me? Where's Kara?"

"She injured her foot."

"Where is she?"

"Indisposed. Where's Francisco?"

"In the van."

"Bring him out."

"Not until I see Kara."

Freddy looked at his watch. "Eleven minutes, twenty-five seconds."

"Excuse me?"

"Not a whole lot of time. She's booby-trapped. An Infernal Explosive Device is hanging around her neck attached to a large pendant. It's due to detonate in exactly twelve minutes and thirty seconds."

I called out. "Kara?"

"He's telling the truth, Buddy. Fucking thing is ticking."

"Free Francisco or she goes blooey," Freddy said. "Your call. Eleven minutes."

I looked at him for a moment, then stepped quickly to the rear of the Explorer. I opened the door and signaled for Francisco to get out.

When he did so, I undid the shackles on his feet, pulled the gag from his mouth and removed his blindfold. I left his hands tied behind his back.

Then I pulled my Glock from its holster and held it on Francisco, who blinked and looked around. He spotted Freddy sitting on top of the Volkswagen.

Freddy nodded to him. He looked at his watch. "Ten and a half minutes exactly."

"Turn off the device and bring Kara out."

"I'm afraid that's not possible."

"You want them both to die?"

"Francisco is going to walk away. Now!" Freddy said.

"I'm going to leave, as well. Then you'll have approximately ten minutes to rescue her. Less if you procrastinate."

Francisco started to inch away.

I made a move to detain him.

Seeing this, Freddy jumped down from atop the Volkswagen, firing his Beretta in my direction as he did.

I dove to the pavement.

Francisco scurried away and ducked behind one of the parked cars.

———

From the roof of the rec center, Petey Brigham watched everything. Although he couldn't hear what was being said, when he saw Francisco bolt, Petey found him in his sights.

Francisco was heading away from the scene, stealthily juking in and out between parked cars.

Petey fired. The windshield of one of the cars exploded, the shot narrowly missing Francisco.

Realizing he was under fire, Francisco ran.

Petey spotted him between two of the cars and fired again.

Francisco was hit. He stumbled and fell. He landed behind one of the cars and stopped moving.

Petey grinned.

———

I rolled into a crouch, partially hidden from Freddy, who knelt beside the Volkswagen, still firing the Beretta.

In his position on the ground, I was able to sight him.

When I saw him hastily changing the Beretta's clip, I made tracks for him.

Seeing me approach, Freddy trained his pistol on me.

Suddenly Freddy's chest exploded, forcing him to windmill backward, like a man attempting to prevent himself from falling.

Petey shot him, I realized.

Freddy stopped and stood stock-still for a moment, trying to grasp what just happened.

He looked in my direction.

"Fuck you," he bellowed.

Then he pitched forward, falling face-first onto the pavement.

I ran to the Volkswagen, scurried up the passenger side door, and jumped down beside Kara.

We stared at each other.

"Don't let me die this way, Buddy."

I looked at the device hanging around her neck. A red light was blinking on its face. I saw the digital number 7.

I searched the device for a turn-off switch. I couldn't find one.

The number on the device changed to 6.

I examined the pendant on which the device was hanging.

I pulled Freddy's stiletto switchblade, the one Shelley had earlier given me, from my pocket. I snapped open the blade and attempted to insinuate it between the chain and Kara's neck.

The device was now displaying the number 5.

Kara's eyes reflected her terror.

I moved the stiletto blade gingerly toward the inside of the pendant, fearful of slicing Kara's neck in the process.

"Just cut it," she said.

I aligned the blade's edge to the chain.

4.

I attempted to sever the chain.

It held.

I tried to cut it a second time, this time with greater effort.

The pendant snapped.

The device slipped down Kara's neck.

I grabbed it.

3, the light read.

Holding it in my hand, I attempted to pull myself out of the Volkswagen.

I couldn't do it with one hand.

I put the device in my pocket and yanked myself up and out of the vehicle.

Once on top, I struggled to reach back and grab hold of the device.

2.

Clumsily, I somehow managed to drop it.

I jumped to the ground and picked it up.

1.

Underhanded, I tossed it between two of the parked cars nearby.

I scurried aboard the Volkswagen, lowered myself onto the driver's seat, and covered Kara's body with my own.

Just as I did, the device exploded in a shower of metal and flames.

Shock waves reverberated, causing the windows of the parked cars to crack and in some cases, shatter.

The front window of the minibus blew out, leaving a residue of flying bits of debris and broken glass.

The noise from the explosion rang in our ears.

Then there was quiet.

——

Atop the rec center, Petey Brigham witnessed the explosion.

Nonetheless, he remained on alert.

He soon spotted one of the *soldados* creeping from the bushes, brushing himself off, and heading for the downed Volkswagen, a pistol in his hand.

Petey squeezed off a round, which slammed into the *soldado's* neck. The *hombre* looked up in surprise. Then he collapsed.

——

The explosion at the entrance to the playground had also attracted the attention of the other *soldados*.

In his effort to emerge from hiding, one of them had become entangled in the cactus behind which he had been hiding.

He tried valiantly to extricate himself from the spiny needles that ensnared him, but succeeded only in making matters worse.

Petey watched for a while as the *soldado* continued to wrestle unsuccessfully with the cactus.

"Moron," he thought.

Although his cigar butt was long gone, he still managed to spit a mouthful of juice into the night.

Then he shot the *soldado*.

———

I lifted myself off of Kara and looked at her. She appeared stricken.

I started to brush the broken glass from us.

"Freddy?" she asked.

"Done for."

"Francisco?"

"Uncertain."

"You?"

"Excuse me?"

She smiled. "You. What took you so long?"

I smiled back.

Shelley exited the Explorer and ran to join us at the Volkswagen.

Stepping over Freddy's body, she called out to me. "You guys okay in there?"

"Never better."

With Shelley's help, I was able to lift Kara out of the minibus and into the front seat of the Explorer.

Then I climbed in beside her.

———

Petey turned his focus to the far side of the playground where he had earlier seen one of Freddy's men secrete himself. Through his night vision goggles, he scoured the area but couldn't spot the *soldado*.

He listened to the quiet for a moment.

He spat.

Then he collected his gear bag and climbed down from atop the rec center.

Once on the ground, he began searching the area.

An errant shot rang out.

Petey dove behind a bench and stared in the direction from which it came.

Another shot.

Petey saw the pistol flash.

He aimed in its direction and fired his rifle.

He heard a thud, then a grunt.

Then he spotted a man running toward him, firing repeatedly in his direction.

A bullet slammed into Petey's chest, and he was thrown backward by its force.

The man kept firing until he had emptied his pistol. Then he stopped running. He stood and gazed at his abdomen. Blood was freely flowing from it. He looked around, as if in search of help.

Then he fell heavily to the ground.

Petey managed to stand, still reeling from the aftermath of the bullet hit.

He slowly approached the fallen man, his rifle pointed at him. As he drew alongside, he saw the man was dead. He lowered his rifle.

He looked at his chest. The Kevlar vest had deflected the shot. But the impact hurt like a son of a bitch.

Petey sucked in his breath and headed for the entrance to the playground where the Explorer was meant to be waiting.

Shelley, Kara, and I watched as he emerged.

Kara pointed him to the back seat.

"Not until I round up Francisco," Petey said as he took off down the street in search of his prey.

He knew he had wounded Francisco but was uncertain as to his fate.

He crept along the row of parked cars, carefully assessing whether or not Francisco was hiding among any of them.

Petey found him downed on the sidewalk adjacent to the park, curled up beside a stone wall, semiconscious.

Francisco was bare-chested, having wrapped his shirt tightly around his thigh, using it as a tourniquet. A bullet wound was oozing blood.

He glanced up as Petey approached him. "I need a doctor," he moaned.

Petey stared for several moments, then strode back to the street, and with waving arms, signaled to Shelley.

When she got to him, Petey struggled Francisco to his feet and hustled him into the Explorer headfirst.

When Petey climbed into the back seat, he found Francisco passed out. His shirt had slipped off the bullet wound and it was now leaking more blood.

As Petey began rewrapping the shirt around Francisco's thigh in an effort to stanch the bleeding, Shelley took off, heading for the Reyes compound.

Once finished with Francisco, Petey took a deep breath and sat back.

He offered greetings to Kara and gave me a thumbs-up. Then he lowered the window and hocked another loogie.

FIFTY-TWO

Upon receiving the go-ahead signal from Doc, Dusty Stengel loaded a rocket into the mouth of his multipurpose assault weapon. He rested it atop his shoulder and took aim at the compound's main gate.

This was a weapon Dusty had a hand in developing, and his knowledge and feel for it were prodigious.

He double- and triple-checked the firing mechanism.

Satisfied, he steadied himself, and, after counting to five, launched the rocket.

The Reyes compound's front gates exploded in a ball of fire.

The burning rocket, having blown through the gates, now hurtled toward the main building, the Paco José house, and landed in a burst of intense flame.

Dusty and Doc charged the compound.

A lone guard appeared at the gate, stunned and disoriented. He was carrying a Beretta model 92 pistol, but Doc took him out before he could pull himself together enough to use it.

They ran to the main house, which was ablaze.

They could hear screams coming from somewhere inside.

They moved in that direction.

———

Shelley pulled into the compound, brakes screeching, and parked beside a small patio located between the two main houses.

I helped Kara out of the Explorer and onto one of the patio benches.

"Which one is the Paco Luis house?" I asked her.

"The one to the right," she said, pointing to it.

"And the one on fire?"

"Paco José's house."

Leaving Francisco on the back seat, Petey jumped from the big SUV and headed toward the fire. Shelley helped settle Kara on the bench.

I left them and raced to the burning building, calling out to Doc and Dusty as I tentatively made my way inside.

I heard a muffled scream and followed the sound. I called out again.

"In here," Doc shouted.

I found him in what appeared to be a private apartment. Flames were climbing the walls and scorching the wooden floor.

An elderly man was seated in a wheelchair. He was having difficulty breathing. The room was hot, and the air was thick with acrid smoke.

Doc was behind the wheelchair, pushing it.

I pitched in and together we managed to get the old man out of the burning building and into the courtyard.

There we spotted Dusty Stengel and his rocket launcher.

Leaving Doc with the wheelchair, I pointed Dusty in the direction of the Paco Luis house, on the far side of the compound.

We found it closed up and locked.

Dusty shot the lock off the front door.

We went inside and set off in search of the basement, the door to which we found in a hallway adjacent to the kitchen.

We opened the door, switched on the lights, and headed downstairs, where we encountered four doors, three of them open.

I shot the lock off the fourth door, and, behind it, we found the crystal meth. Crates of it. All of it bundled and packed, ready for shipping.

I nodded to Dusty. Then we headed back upstairs.

Once at the top, Dusty loaded a rocket into the multipurpose assault weapon and shouldered it.

He aimed it in the direction of the room containing the meth stash.

He fired.

The basement exploded.

We raced out of the building.

———

The entire team had gathered at the patio near the main gate of the compound where Shelley and Kara were waiting.

Shelley breathed a sigh of relief when she saw us approach.

She walked over and stared at me for a long moment.

Then she put her arms around my neck and hugged me.

"That was mighty good work, partner," she said.

I smiled. "I couldn't have done it without you, partner."

When we arrived at the Explorer, I realized Francisco was no longer in the back seat.

"Francisco?" I asked her.

"He slipped out when I was tending to Kara," Shelley sighed. "Sorry."

"Not to worry. He couldn't have gotten very far."

"Does that influence our plan?"

"No."

She smiled. "Then I'll see you in San Diego."

"As long as you drive safely."

"So I was right," she chided.

"About?"

"Your mantra."

"My mantra?"

"Never trust a woman driver," she spouted, a big grin on her face.

"Scram," I admonished.

She gave me a quick hug, jumped into the Explorer, and set off to collect Byron.

———

The old man's wheelchair was positioned beside the bench Kara was occupying.

She had wrapped her foot as best she could but was still clearly in pain.

The old man appeared to have suffered smoke inhalation and was breathing heavily, drifting in and out of consciousness.

"Paco José Reyes," she said, pointing to him.

"The Don?"

"Himself. Currently experiencing respiratory distress."

"And you?"

"Nothing a frozen margarita at Lucy's El Adobe couldn't cure. I'm sorry it had to be this way, Buddy."

"What way?"

"I always pictured seeing you again. But in a more civilized circumstance. You look good."

"Ditto."

"There are so many things I've wanted to tell you. We were so young."

"Shh. It's all okay."

"Really?"

"Really."

"You don't have a load of acrimony toward me?"

"None."

I reached for her hand. She grasped mine and held it to her heart.

I was aware of the impact she had on me. Regardless of the passing of time, I found myself as attracted to her now as I had been when we were together, despite the fact I innately understood it would never happen for us.

"How's the foot?" I asked.

"I'll survive."

Our attention was diverted by an insistent sound that kept growing in intensity.

I looked up in time to see the Boeing Sea Knight dual rotor transport helicopter break through the night sky, drop precipitously, and hover above us.

"Bingo," Doc said.

The bay doors of the helicopter flew open, and a rope net was tossed out and fluttered over our heads.

A pair of Marines scampered quickly down it.

Dusty and Petey began handing their equipment duffels to the Marines, and they in turn handed them to the men in the chopper who were reaching for them.

Once the equipment was loaded, the team began climbing onto the net.

"Time to go," I said to Kara.

I was helping her stand up when the shots rang out. Someone was firing at the helicopter's rotors.

Without waiting for the men to make it aboard, the chopper swiftly lifted off.

Dusty and Doc clung to the net as the Sea Knight raced away from the compound and whomever was trying to bring it down.

My attention was drawn to a noise coming from the nearby bushes.

There I spotted Francisco Reyes emerging from the darkness, a Beretta M9 pistol in his hand.

He moved slowly, limping as he approached us.

Petey's hastily made tourniquet was still wrapped tightly around his thigh. He was in obvious pain.

"Drop your weapon," he hollered hoarsely.

I tossed down my Colt.

He turned to Kara. "I can't believe you did it," he said.

He moved to where my Colt had landed and kicked it aside. His Beretta was still pointed at me.

To Kara he said, "We were so much in love."

"You were so much in love, Frankie."

"Was it all a ruse? Had you no feelings for me?"

She looked away from him.

"You broke my heart," he said.

"You treated me like chattel," she countered. "You lied to me."

"I lied?"

"What rising young Harvard graduate business mogul turned out to be a drug czar?"

"You knew who I was from the beginning."

"Not because you told me."

"I was going to tell you."

"You're full of shit, Frankie."

"You betrayed me, Kara."

"Let's just call it a draw, shall we?" she said.

Francisco stared at me. "Your friends appear to have abandoned you."

Francisco motioned to the Paco Luis house, which was now an inferno.

"You destroyed the meth," he growled. "It had great value."

"And now it doesn't."

"That's where you're wrong. You're about to pay for it with your life. Which makes it very valuable indeed."

I was standing near the Don when I saw Francisco raise his weapon.

I dove behind the wheelchair and in the doing, overturned it, causing the old man to tumble face-first onto the ground.

Francisco glanced down at his fallen father and made a move toward him.

Without warning, Kara, who had been sitting in front of me, tentatively stood and once on her feet, reached into my pocket and grabbed the switchblade. She snapped it open.

Francisco turned his attention to her.

Kara launched herself at him.

Francisco was startled by her move. He turned the Beretta on her, but before he could get off a shot, she smashed into him.

As he reeled backward, Kara drove the stiletto deeply into his heart.

Francisco's eyes widened.

Instinctively he reached for the knife with the intention of pulling it out, but before he could, he groaned and fell forward, his eyes clouding over.

"Kara," he whispered.

He was dead before he hit the ground.

Kara made eye contact with me. She appeared stunned by what she had done.

I was nodding my approval when I noticed movement and

turned in time to see Don Paco José unsteadily remove a pistol from his pocket.

He turned toward Kara and pointed it at her. "You've left me with nothing," he said.

She backed away from him. "It wasn't my choice."

"More of your bullshit, Kara?"

"I never meant you harm."

"Tell your lies to God," he said and shot her.

She fell backward, gasping for breath, clutching her side.

"Suffer," the old man snarled.

I trained my Glock on him and fired.

The shot tore into his chest, ripping a gaping hole in his aorta.

He fell in a heap, the pistol still clutched in his lifeless hand.

I rushed to Kara. Blood was leaking through her fingers. "How bad?"

"I don't know. I can't feel anything."

I tore open her shirt and examined the wound. There was a great deal of blood.

I grabbed the light cotton towel that had laid across the old man's lap, folded it into a square and pressed it to her wound. I told her to hold it as tightly as she could.

Then I pulled out my cell phone and punched in Doc's number.

I knelt beside Kara.

"He's dead?" she asked.

"He was a soulless man," I said.

"He was the Don."

"Don't ascribe nobility to him. He killed scores of people with his drugs. And left hundreds more as good as dead. Him and his son. They were bad people, Kara."

"Sometimes it wasn't so easy for me to see that."

"Ridding the world of them was the right thing," I said.

She looked at me and smiled weakly.

Within minutes the Boeing Sea Knight once again descended. The net was lowered, and both Doc and the team medic scrambled down.

The medic examined Kara, then withdrew a large gauze pad from his emergency kit and taped it tightly to the wound. He administered a morphine injection.

Doc and the medic gently lifted her into the waiting arms of Petey Brigham and Dusty Stengel, who, in turn, handed her to the pair of Marines inside the chopper.

The medic, Doc, and then I, took hold of the net and climbed onto it.

"Go. Go. Go," Doc shouted as we made our way inside.

The Sea Knight lifted off.

When I looked, I caught sight of the burning compound. The methamphetamine had fueled a fire that continued to burn out of control.

I could make out several people gathering in front of the compound and on the beach.

I heard the sound of sirens in the distance.

The big chopper picked up speed as it hurtled upward, away from the fiery remains of the storied Reyes compound.

Soon it leveled and raced with purpose into the dark black night.

FIFTY-THREE

The Sea Knight flew west, across the Gulf of California, over Baja, on a beeline toward the Pacific where it banked north and headed for the heliport atop San Diego's Scripps Mercy Hospital.

Kara was lying on a makeshift surgical table, being tended to by the medic. He initiated a fluid drip. The morphine helped her withstand the pain.

I sat beside her, holding her hand.

She was experiencing the effects of the drug. Her speech slurred. Her eyes drifted in and out of focus. "Where are we going?" she asked.

"San Diego. We should be there in twenty minutes."

"Will I live?"

"To a ripe old age."

"Be serious."

"I am serious. You're in very good hands."

"Can you forgive me?"

"For what?"

"My broken foot. Getting shot."

"Have you always been this accident prone?"

She smiled weakly. "How did you do it?"

"Do what?"

"Follow me to Mexico."

"We drove."

"You know what I mean. LAPD has no jurisdiction in a foreign territory."

"Better you not know. That way you'll have plausible deniability."

She nodded off for a while.

Then her eyes suddenly opened. "I got caught up in it," she murmured. "It was very intense. One day I was an employee, the next I was living like royalty with Francisco. It was more than I bargained for. It happened so fast."

I reached over and moved a stray lock of hair from her forehead.

"He couldn't get enough of me," she said. "I went everywhere with him. I was treated like family. Then the shit hit the fan. I became a pariah."

"Is that when I saw you?"

"Something had gone wrong. Suddenly I was being closely watched. I was denied outside access. Guards buzzed around me like sand flies. I still don't know exactly what happened."

"To the best of our ability to interpret what we learned, it appears as if one of our agents turned."

"Turned?"

"Went rogue."

"And?"

"He allegedly informed Freddy there was someone on the inside. A spy. He offered to trade that person's identity for a significant payday."

"Then why were they so uncertain about me?"

"Because Freddy slipped up and killed the informant."

"Before he gave up my name?"

"Our guy must have had second thoughts. He clammed up."

"And Freddy couldn't weasel the information out of him?"

I shrugged. "Looks like it."

She nodded off again.

The medic checked her fluid intake and her IV. He looked at his watch. "Less than ten minutes."

"How's she doing?"

"She's stabilized. There's a surgical team standing by."

Kara's eyes flickered open. She looked up at me, smiled, and then lowered her eyes. "We were kids, Buddy. We were a fantasy. It would never have worked for us. I'm doomed to be a loner."

The Sea Knight was banking right. The lights of San Diego came into view.

"Please don't think poorly of me, Buddy."

I leaned over and kissed the top of her head. I could smell the sea in her hair. Her familiar closeness brought a tightness to my chest.

"I could never think poorly of you, Kara. I admire your courage and bravery."

The Sea Knight touched gently down atop Mercy Hospital. The rotors spun to a stop. The bay doors opened and a swarm of medical personnel came aboard and hovered around her.

Then they lifted the gurney. She looked back at me as they lowered her to the ground.

I watched them race her inside.

FIFTY-FOUR

Doc and I stood together on the tarmac. The night air was clean and crisp. We were engulfed by the swirling breezes that blew in from the Pacific. Banks of light towers illuminated the area.

There was a great deal of activity around the helicopter. Hospital personnel and vehicles came and went. It was just after three a.m.

"I'm gonna stick around here for a while," I said.

"I understand," Doc said. "Next weekend?"

"Golf?"

"Of course golf. Palm Springs or Vegas?"

"Palm Springs."

"I can probably keep the guys around on one pretext or another."

"Can you get the big house?"

"You have to ask that question?"

"I need to know whether to pack for luxury or Motel 6."

"You don't own anything geared for luxury."

"If I did."

"Friday?"

"I'm there."

Doc nodded and turned toward the chopper. Then he looked back. "You did good, Buddy."

"You, too, Doc."

We exchanged a brief hug.

Doc climbed aboard the Sea Knight.

Petey and Dusty waved to me from inside, flashing the thumbs-up sign.

Everyone cleared the tarmac and watched as the big bird lifted off and disappeared into the night sky.

I followed the surgical team into the hospital and settled myself in the waiting room where I phoned Shelley and Byron to tell them what had gone down.

They had already crossed the border and promised to join me shortly.

Then I leaned back in my chair and closed my eyes.

———

The first vestiges of daylight had become visible in the gray sky when the surgeon stepped into the waiting room, where he found Shelley, Byron, and me, sprawled out on various pieces of furniture. I looked up when he entered.

"She's a lucky woman," Dr. Gale Kennedy, the surgeon, said. "Bullet went straight through her, somehow managing to miss anything vital. We sewed her up pretty good. She'll make a full recovery."

"May I see her?" I asked.

"Only for a moment."

After a brief glance at Shelley and Byron, I followed Dr. Kennedy into the recovery room.

Kara was alone, hooked up to a rash of IVs and machines. She was asleep.

"Only a moment," Dr. Kennedy said.

I stepped to the side of her bed. I reached down and took her hand. Her eyes fluttered open.

"You're doing great, Kara."

"Am I okay?"

"You'll be as good as new in no time. Better, even."

She squeezed my hand.

Dr. Kennedy cleared her throat.

"I have to go," I said.

"Will I see you again?"

"Margaritas at Lucy's. On me."

"Really?"

"I promise."

Her smiling eyes closed.

I stepped away from the bed, shook hands with Dr. Kennedy, gathered Shelley and Byron, and together we left the hospital.

———

We pulled into Pendleton just after six a.m. where we were met by a Marine warrant officer who helped us transfer our luggage from the Sonoran rental into a waiting limousine.

We settled in, and the limo pulled out for the two-hour drive to Los Angeles.

We were silent for a while, each of us savoring his or her own thoughts, each relaxing for the first time following a week of high stress and anxiety.

"I could never get it right," I said.

"Get what right?" Shelley asked.

"The joke I keep wanting to make."

"What joke?" Byron asked.

"The Shelley and Byron joke."

"Excuse me?" Byron said.

"Mary Shelley and Lord Byron."

"What about them?"

Shelley snorted.

"What?" Byron said.

"Mary Shelley and Lord Byron," I said. "The literary duo."

"Huh," Byron said.

Then, after several moments, he said, "Oh, I get it."

"Too late."

"It's a bit obscure, don't you think?"

"For your average dolt perhaps."

"Oh come on. I mean who even knows who those German writers were?"

"English."

"What?"

"English. They were English."

"Whatever," Byron said.

Nobody spoke for a while.

"Where are we going?" Byron asked finally.

"Parker Center."

"For what?"

"Debriefing would be my guess."

"You mean they won't let us get some sleep before they run us through the wringer?"

"If you'd quit bellyaching, we might get some sleep on the way there."

"You're kidding, right? Who can sleep in a moving vehicle?"

"I can," Shelley said.

"Me too," I said.

Before too much longer, Byron was the only one of us still awake.

"The Shelley and Byron joke," he muttered to himself. "Stupid."

FIFTY-FIVE

We arrived at Parker Center at eight thirty. After stashing our bags with the desk sergeant, we headed for Commander Jeremy Logan's office.

The frantic activity of the early days of the riots had abated. Los Angeles was approaching normal. The curfew was about to be lifted. Cleanup crews and police officers had returned to the streets of South Central. Businesses were reopening.

The LAPD bigwigs were just now standing down.

When Byron, Shelley, and I entered his office, we found Logan and Murray Goodman. Both of them stood to greet us.

A giant coffee urn and a tray of pastries were on hand, and the three of us helped ourselves generously.

"There goes my diet," Shelley said.

"Mine too," Logan said as he reached for a cheese Danish.

"Shall we get down to it?" Goodman said.

"Why waste time with pleasantries?" I snickered.

"Okay. Okay," Logan said. "Allow me to welcome you back and to thank you. You've done us a great service for which we are enormously grateful. I'm thinking a day of rest might be in order before you begin the debriefing ordeal. How about we schedule you for tomorrow?"

The three of us nodded our assent.

"That was quite a rescue," the commander said.

"We got lucky," I said.

"Didn't appear as luck to me."

"Despite a surprise or two, it went pretty much as we planned."

"My point exactly," Logan said. "Luck is the residue of design. Your design was pretty damn good."

He stood, and everyone took that as their cue. "Thank you again," Logan said and shook hands with each of us. "After the debriefing tomorrow, I think you should take a holiday."

"Wow," Byron said.

We all filed out of the office. When I reached the door, Logan stopped me.

"Stay for a moment," he said. I hung back.

He wandered over and closed the door. "Very impressive, Buddy. Beyond the call."

"Have you heard anything more about Kara?"

"She's still in intensive care, but they expect a full recovery. Once she's well enough, she'll be debriefed by the Feds. You caught us an amazing break when you destroyed the meth. After what we've just been through, having to face a significant narcotics influx would have freighted us immeasurably."

"We can thank Doc's team for that."

"We can thank you for that."

"It was a team effort, sir."

"Go take some time for yourself, Buddy. Get off it for a while. Then come see me."

We stood and shook hands.

"Do you remember what I told you when all this began?"

"Yes, sir."

"Well, again, this is just the start. You have a big future, Buddy. I'm very proud of you."

Then, with his arm wrapped around my shoulder and a big grin on his face, he walked me to the door.

FIFTY-SIX

I arrived at Capra's Haven early, purposefully ahead of when my mother was expected.

The resort-like complex of twenty-five assisted-living apartments was located in the Los Feliz section of Los Angeles county, adjacent to Griffith Park.

Betty Jean and Jimmy were already there when I pulled in. We greeted each other with hugs and smiles.

"Jimmy deserves a medal," Betty Jean offered. "The minute she boarded the tour bus, he was with me inside her room. He helped pack it up in record time."

"Way to go, Jimmy," I said, clapping him on the back. He grinned.

"How did you get her on the tour bus?" I inquired as we stood in front of the building complex. "Especially since it left from here."

"Easy. She claimed never to have seen Universal before." Betty Jean said. "And more importantly, we slipped her a flask filled with her favorite single malt whiskey before she boarded."

"Sweet," I said.

"She's due back in about an hour," she said. "So Jimmy and

I have just enough time to unpack her stuff before she gets here."

"Amazing," I said.

"I'm so grateful he was willing to help," Betty Jean said.

"Come on, Mom," Jimmy said. "Of course I was willing to help. Jeez."

"And Cooper?" I asked Jimmy.

"In the car. Now it'll be my turn to miss him."

The big bloodhound was beside himself when I attached the leash to his collar.

He could barely contain himself when we set off to explore the grounds.

The owner of the facility, Brandie Capra, had innately understood the therapeutic value of canine companions for senior residents.

As was the protocol, Cooper underwent the equivalent of an audition in front of the Haven's staff. He passed with flying colors.

All that remained now was for my mom to make her appearance and sanction the move, a totally unexpected one.

Cooper and I spent the hour nosing around. The grounds were spacious and ecologically sound. Heritage oaks dotted the landscape, which was also host to a myriad of leafy bushes and colorfully blossoming trees.

We joined Jimmy and Betty Jean inside what was to become my mother's ground-floor suite of rooms. Although small, the apartment boasted a kitchen/dining area, a living room complete with two sofas, a love seat, and a large-screen TV, as well as an ample bedroom/bathroom combo.

It had a small patio that offered views of the grounds and welcomed the fragrant breezes that engulfed the complex.

We were all present when Mom was escorted inside by Ms. Capra.

She was at first confused and a bit overwhelmed.

Especially when Cooper nearly knocked her down as he raced to her side.

When she saw me, my mother exclaimed, "What in the hell is going on here?"

"Welcome home, Mom," I said.

With that, both Betty Jean and Jimmy applauded.

"Home?" she exclaimed.

"Home," I said. "Have a look."

With that, Ms. Capra echoed our welcome and left us. Betty Jean led Mom and Cooper on a tour.

Finding all of her belongings already there, along with Cooper, she queried again, "What in the hell is going on here?"

"We moved you," I said.

"Moved me?"

"Yep. Now you get to live in this wonderful assisted-living facility. And with Cooper too."

"My goodness," she exclaimed.

"I suspect your goodness vanished some time ago," I needled her. "But now you get to live as you've wanted."

She looked at us all.

"You arranged this for me, Buddy?"

I shrugged.

"He did," Betty Jean said.

"How lucky I am," she exclaimed.

Which is when first she, and then I, broke into tears.

POSTSCRIPT

SUNDAY, JUNE 16, 2022

As I pulled on my one good suit and prepared myself for the drive south to LA and his funeral, I realized anew that my career in law enforcement was built largely on the foundation of Jeremy Logan's faith and confidence in me.

I wasn't alone in my admiration of him.

When Byron Prescott had phoned to inform me of the event and invite me to join him, he advised we get there early because they were expecting a record-setting crowd.

"Doc and the guys will be joining us," Byron said.

"Kara?" I asked.

"Surprise," he said.

"What surprise?"

"I found her."

"Found her where?"

"I'm not sure she wants me to tell you."

"Tell me."

"I just said…"

"I know what you just said. Tell me."

After several moments, he said, "Frisco."

"She's in San Francisco?"

Byron didn't say anything. "Number?" I asked.

"I told her I wouldn't give it to you."

"Number," I said again.

"She's not going to like it."

"And you care about what she likes?"

He gave me the number.

"*Gracias*," I said.

Byron ignored my remark. "Fans and nonfans alike are going to be there. Most of them saddened by his passing. Several others, though, appear to be elated. Hopefully no fistfights will break out."

"Fistfights at a funeral?"

"Not just any funeral," Byron said. "Let's not forget whose life we're honoring."

Byron's assessment stayed with me. Even as I was dialing her number.

"Machado," she answered.

"Steel," I offered.

Silence.

Then, several seconds later, "Buddy?"

"Yep."

"Oh my God," she stammered.

"Hello, Kara."

"Byron, right?"

"Yep."

"I knew I shouldn't have told him."

"Aren't you glad to hear from me, Kara? I know I'm glad."

"Where are you?"

"Freedom, California."

"Married?"

"What are you, nuts?"

"Me neither."

"So what's stopping us?"

"From?"

"Don't play dumb, Kara."

"When is it?"

"The funeral?"

"Yes."

"Tomorrow," I told her.

"Okay."

"Okay, what?"

"What would happen if I was there?"

"It's anyone's guess."

"What's your guess?"

"I'm guessing I could get lucky."

"You're such a jerk, Buddy."

"I'll see you tomorrow," I said and ended the call.

I sat stunned for several minutes.

Once again Jeremy Logan had succeeded in impacting my life. Ol' one-of-a-kind Logan.

That's how I'll always remember him.

Benevolent yet divisive.

One of a kind.

God bless you, Jeremy.

I'll cherish your memory for as long as I live.

Rest in peace, old friend.

Read on for an excerpt from
RISK FACTOR
another exciting Buddy Steel Thriller!

ONE

The first place they hit was my father's house.

The Sheriff and my stepmother, Regina Goodnow, the mayor of Freedom Township, discovered the break-in when they returned from a Palm Springs weekend.

The thieves had grabbed whatever small valuables were lying around, including some of Regina's cherished jewelry and a pair of antique watches. They swept the bathroom clean of prescription medications. They cracked the master bedroom's hidden wall safe and ransacked it.

The police surmised it was the work of burglars who had recently pillaged a number of upscale homes in the Santa Barbara area.

They appeared to have had knowledge of the layout of the house. They were expert in disarming the security alarm system. None of the neighbors had seen nor heard anything out of the ordinary.

At the time, I was on a sabbatical. Time spent away from the San Remo Sheriff's Department, where I had been working alongside my father as his deputy.

No sooner had the old man been elected to a third term as

County Sheriff than he was diagnosed with ALS, Amyotrophic Lateral Sclerosis, aka Lou Gehrig's disease.

When he continued to respond positively to a new pharmaceutical that promised to slow the progress of the disease, everyone breathed a sigh of relief.

I took it as my cue to grab some much-needed downtime in which to rest, reinvigorate, reevaluate, and pay heed to my own psychological well-being.

I am currently in Deer Valley, Utah, in a rustic cabin that belongs to Jordyn Yates, who is not only my attorney, but also a woman with whom I'm sharing a newly rejuvenated romance.

By way of introduction, my name is Buddy Steel. Actually it's Burton Steel Jr. I'm a thirty-three-year-old law enforcement professional, currently experiencing what might be termed a midlife meltdown.

Footloose, seeking answers to questions I've yet to even formulate, I'd spent the last several weeks beachcombing the Mexican coastline from Cancun to the Riviera Maya.

Now, in search of a breath of non-salty air, I am enjoying the rugged peaks and canyons of the Wasatch Mountain range, whose sharp ridgelines stand watch over verdant fields and Alpine lakes that were originally formed by ancient, Pleistocene-era glaciers.

Because I had been off the grid for a while, the ringing of my cell phone startled me.

"Buddy," I answered.

"Is that you?" Captain Marsha Russo of the San Remo County Sheriff's office responded.

"Marsha?"

"Buddy?"

"Yes."

"It's really you."

"Was there a reason for this call, Marsha?"

"Are you sitting down?"

"What is it?"

"Your family manse was hit last night."

"Meaning?"

"Burglary. High-end professional job. Upset the old man terribly."

"Meaning?"

"He wants you."

"In what way?"

"In the '*I Need Buddy To Come Home*' way. '*Immediately.*'"

"Shit."

"I knew you'd say that."

"What were his exact words?"

"'*Locate him and get his ass back here.*'"

"That's what he said?"

"More than once. And I omitted the profanities."

"Tell him you can't find me."

"No."

"What, no? Just tell him I didn't answer my phone."

"May I say something in confidence, Buddy?"

"What?"

"You're fucked. How soon can you be here?"

TWO

It took more than half a day to make the drive, and I pulled the Wrangler into the garage of my condo in Freedom sometime after two a.m. I showed up at the office at ten.

I was in the throes of determining just how depressed I was when Marsha stepped into my office and dropped down in one of the two visitor's chairs. "You don't look any different."

I gave her my best dead-eyed stare. "Where is he?"

"It's nice to have you back, Buddy."

"Let's not get ahead of ourselves here, okay? Nobody said I was back."

She flashed me a crooked grin. "He's at the house. With Johnny Kennerly. It hit him hard."

"The break-in?"

"And the loss of his stuff."

"The safe?"

"Lots of valuable stuff in such a small safe."

"Such as?"

"Wills. Deeds. Titles. Plus a bundle of cash."

"Replaceable?"

"That's an insurance company question. But the vulnerability proved difficult for them."

"Them being himself and Her Honor?"

"You're so perceptive, Buddy."

"You were saying…"

"We're seeing a bunch of similar home invasions. Most recently in Santa Barbara County. Now here. All targeting the rich and famous."

"He knows I'm in town?"

"He can hardly contain himself."

"Shit."

"How did I know you'd come to that realization?"

———

My father and the mayor live in one of the more upscale neighborhoods of Freedom, the two of them puttering around the creaky old mansion in which I grew up.

As I climbed the steps to the front porch, my thoughts were of my late mother. I knew when I stepped inside I'd be confronted with the reality that everything which reflected her personal tastes and interests had either been overhauled or replaced by my stepmother.

But in that brief instant, after ringing the bell and waiting for the door to open, I fantasized I would be entering the cherished dwelling of my youth. Exactly as it had been.

"Buddy," Regina pronounced as she enveloped me in a bear hug.

She wore a modest blue suit, a gray silk T-shirt, and a look of grave concern.

She gave me the once-over. "You don't look any more rested or relaxed for all your highfalutin gallivanting."

"Nice to see you, too, Regina."

She closed the door behind us. "He's with Johnny."

She led me to the kitchen, which had come to serve as her

in-house operations center. "Can I get you anything?" she asked as she pointed me to a seat at the large, round, polished-oak table that dominated the room.

"I'm good. Thanks."

She sat across from me, in front of a pile of papers and a half-empty coffee mug. "This has upset him terribly."

"Tell me."

"He's always considered the house inviolate. His castle, so to speak. His refuge. The break-in and thefts shattered that image. He hasn't been the same since we discovered it."

At that moment my father stormed into the kitchen, followed by his longtime protégé and current deputy, Johnny Kennerly, a large man of color who was totally devoted to him.

"I told you I heard voices," he tossed over his shoulder to Johnny.

He briefly embraced me, then gave me the once-over. "You need a haircut."

I exchanged smiles with Johnny.

"Good time?" he inquired.

"Better than a good time."

"You look great."

"I feel great."

My father sneered. "How much longer will this bromance hooyah go on?"

"Nothing changes," I said to Johnny.

"Tell me about it. While you were away finding yourself, I was here. With him."

"Grim?"

"Worse."

"This is like a fucking episode of *The Real Housewives of New Jersey*," my father snarled to Regina.

"Burton, please..." she replied.

Acknowledgments

My gratitude and appreciation for the support and assistance provided by my cherished team of contributors.

My devotion and indebtedness to the late, great Joan and Robert B. Parker.

Thank you, Michael Barson.

Thanks to Dominique Raccah and the Sourcebooks group.

Thanks also to Beth Deveny, for her sharp-eyed edit of the manuscript.

Special thanks to the brilliant Diane DiBiase, whose invaluable expertise and insight so formidably enriched the narrative.

My gratitude to the team of advance readers who always spot all that I miss: Steven Brandman, Miles Brandman, David Chapman, and Roy Gnan.

Much appreciation for the support of my longtime friend and partner, Tom Selleck.

Special kudos to Tom Distler, for his encouragement and rock-solid counsel.

And my profound love for my late brother, Jeffrey, and for our departed parents, Selma and Arthur Brandman.

Thank you, one and all.

About the Author

Photo by Joanna Miles

Michael Brandman is the author of three Jesse Stone novels, each based on characters created by Robert B. Parker, all on the *New York Times* bestsellers list.

With his longtime partner, Tom Selleck, he produced and cowrote nine Jesse Stone movies and three Westerns.

His and Emanuel Azenberg's production of Tom Stoppard's *Rosencrantz & Guildenstern Are Dead* won the Venice Film Festival's Golden Lion Award for Best Picture.

He has produced more than forty motion pictures, including films written by Arthur Miller, Stephen Sondheim, Neil Simon, David Mamet, Horton Foote, Wendy Wasserstein, David Hare, and Athol Fugard.

He is the father of two sons and lives in Los Angeles with his wife, the actress Joanna Miles.